Finding Grace

FINDING GRACE

Stories by

KURT RHEINHEIMER

Jefferson Madison
Regional Library
Charlottesville, Virginia

Press 53
Winston-Salem

Press 53, LLC
PO Box 30314
Winston-Salem, NC 27130

First Edition

Copyright © 2012 by Kurt Rheinheimer

All rights reserved, including the right of reproduction in whole or in part in any form except in the case of brief quotations embodied in critical articles or reviews. For permission, contact author at editor@Press53.com, or at the address above.

Cover design by Kevin Morgan Watson

Cover art, "The Wheelbarrow," Copyright © 2012 by Matt Hunter, used by permission of the artist.

Library of Congress Control Number: 2012906104

This is a work of fiction. Names, characters, places, and incidents are products of the author's imagination or are used fictionally. Any resemblance to actual events, locales, or persons, living or dead, is entirely coincidental.

Printed on acid-free paper
ISBN 978-1-935708-58-2

*For my father, Walter Heinrich Rheinheimer,
and my late mother, Mildred Eloise Hurt*

Acknowledgments

Many of the stories in *Finding Grace* first appeared in the following publications:

"Clothespins" and "I Saw My Mother Today," *Raleigh News & Observer*

"New Weather" and "Sirens," *Black Warrior Review*

"Concussions," *Glimmer Train*

"Dirt," *Indiana Review*

"Key Box," *Potomac Review*

"The Lake," *The Sun*

"Cold," *2010 Press 53 Open Awards Anthology*

"A Short History of the Stamps," *Shenandoah*

"Kentucky Moon," *American Literary Review*

"New Weather" won the Black Warrior Review Fiction Award

Finding Grace

Preface: The Honey Moon	xi
Clothespins	1
New Weather	5
Concussions	13
Sirens	25
Dirt	37
Key Box	51
The Lake	67
Cold	81
Soup for Cannon	95
A Short History of the Stamps	105
Kentucky Moon	119
Motherless Children	143
I Saw My Mother Today	153

Preface: The Honey Moon

It's a perfectly clear late afternoon in October, with the moon low, near-full and see-through white against the blue. They are in and out of that day, my parents, through the screen door from the kitchen. Only some of the honey has been put into jars. They carry samples of the sweet, light locust honey, one at a time out into the daylight, to hold them against the sun as if protecting their eyes to watch an eclipse, and look through the honey for clarity and lightness and balance, for perfection—in preparation for the state fair in two days.

You could step slightly farther out into the yard than they, into the shade of the holly tree, and look up and down Oak Drive—at a dozen houses in each direction, all exactly like theirs—and you would see no one else outside in the late sun. It is Thursday, and the women are inside with their children, preparing suppers of pork chops or meatloaf. The men are at work, most of them at the aircraft company that built these houses for its workers and their families.

They are thirty-four and twenty-six, Edwin and Grace. His parents are in downtown Baltimore and hers in Southwestern Virginia. Their first child is four years old, standing on his bed and looking out the window, though not particularly at his parents, who are, on this day in 1950, alone together in the best way two people can be, enlivened by the crisp air, the honey, their life.

Yet no one—not even they—records this moment in any way. It is simply a piece of a day of life, a day in a small, war-built neighborhood northeast of Baltimore, a day apparent to no one as any different from the one before or the one to come, or from hundreds and thousands on either side of it.

But that day could be marked, as every day could, for what we will be able to see from the perspective of twenty or forty or sixty years later, as having been noteworthy after all. We'd look at them so differently if we could—today—watch these motions in the yard in the afternoon, so many decades back. Are there rings on their fingers? Do they pause and look at each other for the sake of looking at each other? Does Grace's face carry the first tint of the irritation that will grow in her over the years from the sticky mess of the process of making honey in their kitchen? Is Edwin so beautifully naive that he sees nothing but the clear honey in the jar and the pretty face of his wife?

It is the arc of life that is the greatest miracle, and it is our inability to see the minutes of the arc—as we cannot see the steps that slowly turn pure, transparent honey to a thick, opaque crystallized mass—that is our greatest failing. These stories all have their geneses in visions and images of Edwin and Grace that did not register as they were witnessed, but which presented themselves, somewhere long past the time when the tiny, intricate workings of hearts accrued as invisibly as heartbeats themselves—occurring unseen, unacknowledged and at the same frequency as the passing of hours—to create the arc.

CLOTHESPINS

Grace is out on the mild slope of the front yard. The grass is wet with heavy dew as she stands in small, white-canvas shoes. She wears cotton turquoise shorts and a blouse that is faded and thin, a creamish color with short sleeves and three buttons down the front. She carries clothespins in her mouth. Beside her, steam rises off a round wicker basket full of just-washed clothes.

You look up at the sky, so brilliantly blue and high and uncomplicated, that seems to go on forever, seems to envelop her with perfect clear protection, to arch over her with a warming embrace even in the coolness of the early summer morning.

When she has one line full of clothes and another half full, the Willys comes down Oak Drive. The combination of the big rough tires and the rough black pavement creates a strong, masculine noise into the early morning. The Willys is squarish, halfcar/halftruck, painted gray with parts of its sides painted a darker gray. It looks like government surplus to her.

Edwin makes the turn onto Fourth Road and runs

the Willys into the little muddy ruts at the bottom of the slope where Grace is hanging the clothes. He turns the engine off. It runs for several more seconds and then stops as he opens the door. The door squeaks loudly into the quiet morning. He steps out slowly, a small, blocky man in his thirties. He is nearly bald. He has on greenish shorts, a white t-shirt and bulky socks and hiking boots. His legs are hairy, thick looking.

"Hi," he says.

"Hello," Grace says. "Fancy meeting you here." Because of the clothespins in her mouth, it comes out, "Antsy weating wu here."

He walks carefully around the edge of the yard to the sidewalk, instead of coming up the hill through the grass. He walks slowly while Grace goes back to clothes hanging. He has to be at work in a little more than an hour.

When he is most of the way up the walk to the house, he speaks again. "Grace."

She turns, a surprised look on her face as three clothespins stick out of her mouth. "Wesh?"

He moves across the grass toward her. When he is a few feet away she sees his face begin to crush together in the middle. He is crying by the time he reaches her. She has never seen him cry. She takes the clothespins from her mouth and moves to meet him. He pushes his face into her shoulder and sobs.

"What?" she says, "what is it?" Her arms are held lightly around his back. There are clothespins in one hand, sticking out like extra fingers. His back is sticky. He smells like wax and bees and honey. He smells like their house. They have not been able to use the sink for weeks because he has frames from his hives in there, and the honey extractor up on the counter next to the sink. And sticky liquid all over the counter where there should be fancy dishes and containers of flour and sugar.

"What?" she says again.
"I fell asleep," he says into her collarbone. "I mean I must have. I was driving Cubby Knob Road there in the county, with the last load of hives, and then I didn't know anything until I was running right along a little creek, far into a field." He sobs.
"In a field?" she says.
"Way way in," he says. "Maybe two hundred yards, and I was driving through brush up to the windshield almost—just cutting right through it."
"It wasn't a dream?"
His body convulses again before he tells her it was a nightmare.
"But you woke up?"
"I guess the bumping and the noise of the brush against the side of the car did it. But then it was like a dream. I had no idea where I was or what I was doing for a few seconds. And then just before I would have gone into the stream, I realized things and put the brakes on. And then she stalled. In all that brush there, with the bees all upset from all the jostling."
She looks down toward the Willys. It looks undamaged, unchanged. It always looks scratched and muddy. There are no hives in the back.
"But you got out?"
He lifts his head from her shoulder. "It took some time, but she started and I backed out just the way I came in—backed over the same brush. It took a long long time."
"And the bees ended up okay?"
"They seemed to calm down." He rubs at the upper parts of his cheeks with the tips of his fingers.
"You need to start moving the bees on the weekend instead of at night," she says. "Get more sleep."
"The orchard needs them when the orchard needs

them," he says. He turns and starts toward the house. She watches him, looks again at the Willys, then at the laundry. She puts clothespins back into her mouth and hangs the rest of the laundry. When she is finished she glances up at the high blue sky, as if to judge how quickly it will dry her clothes.

Edwin has taken a bath, eaten eggs and gone to work before their little son awakens. As Edwin leaves—preparing to aim the Willys back up Oak Drive to the aircraft factory where he drills holes for rivets in airplane bodies—Grace watches. She watches him back the Willys from Fourth onto Oak, turn back sharply toward the sidewalk, and then head up Oak. He doesn't turn to look at her as he passes the house. He has no concept of waving as he goes. This is a direct, straightforward, practical man, her husband. She has never told her mother that he was born in Germany and came to the United States when he was a little boy. The crying over falling asleep is the strangest, most intimate thing he has ever done with her. But now he is on his way to work, gone again.

Out on the slope of the yard, the clothes give off the last of their steamy heat as the sun begins to dry the dew off the grass. The neighborhood awakens and Grace begins to prepare another set of eggs—these for her and Alex. She will not think to tell him about what happened to his father, and soon she will take Alex out into the yard to play in the little cleared spot where his toy trucks are, near the end of the clothesline, under the brilliant, guiltless blue sky above them all.

New Weather

In the night there was a big rainstorm that blew the remaining leaves off the trees and brought the tide up over some of the piers in the cove. The sewers flooded and floated leaves onto the street and sidewalk. Now it is Saturday morning and the air is much cooler, with big clouds moving across a deep blue sky. My father is working on his Studebaker. It is a 1948 red Champion convertible and he is doing something to the engine. He wears old dress pants that shine at the seat as he bends over the fender. I am on my tricycle, moving it slowly over the mat of shiny brown leaves on the sidewalk. Some of the leaves stick to the big front wheel and ride up until they hit the fender and fall off. My head is covered with white bandages to protect the spot where Sylvia Jackson hit me with a rock on Monday, after I threw her toy frog onto the roof of her house. They took me to the hospital in the Jacksons' Buick. I bled onto my mother's dress and the front seat of the Buick.

My mother comes out of the house carrying a basket of steamy laundry. She walks carefully across the wet yard to the lines that are near the edge of the yard. The wind blows her hair back and forth in front of her face. She wears red slacks that stop at the middle of her calves, and a light blue jacket and white tennis shoes with tiny holes near the little toes. I move the tricycle up the sidewalk toward her for a distance, looking behind to see if I leave tracks. When I look back toward the car, my father is raised up from the hood, and is looking up the street. He goes back to the engine for a second and then he stares up the street again. Far up Oak, across from the baseball diamond, there is an old man in a dark suit, walking slowly down the sidewalk. I turn my tricycle around toward my father, to watch the man. At first I think it is the blind man who lives at the end of our street. But it is the wrong time of day for him to be walking down the street. And this man is not carrying a white cane. My father is standing straight up now.

"Grace," he says, without turning toward my mother. She takes a clothespin out of her mouth and looks up the street, and then I see that it is my grandfather, on the way to visit. It is the wrong grandfather—not the one in Virginia, but the one we go to visit sometimes on Sundays. I have never seen him at our house. He lives in a dark cold house that smells like a wet couch. It is downtown near the stadium. Sometimes when we go to visit, he stays behind the gray curtain that separates the living room and the bedroom. My grandmother sits alone with us in the living room, rubbing her hands over each other again and again. On other Sundays, my grandfather comes out from behind the curtain and plays the violin. On the way home from the visits, my mother and father talk about how he was doing that day. The talks and the gray curtain and the odd smell have taught me to be afraid of my grandfather.

When he is just up the sidewalk from the Studebaker,

my grandfather says, "Good morning, good morning, good morning," with a little bow toward each one of us. He speaks with an accent that I think has to do with old age and the way he is on Sundays. His suit is dark wool. He wears a white shirt, and a tie with brown and blue stripes. His hair is white and tufty, like a chicken's, and the little silver hairs on his chin and cheeks glisten in the sunlight.

"Trouble with the Studebaker?" he says. He pronounces it "Stootabecka." My father has told me that he and my grandmother and grandfather came over from Germany in a boat, when he was just a little older than I am now. I have no image of my father on a tricycle.

"What do you want?" my father says, still standing straight up. My father is exactly the same height as my grandfather, and has the same little ball at the end of his nose.

"How's the head?" my grandfather says to me, and puts out his hand. "You have to be careful with the women, you know, Alex." He holds my hand for a second between his thumb and first two fingers.

"Fine," I say, turning to look for my mother. My grandfather seems bigger and even more frightening than he has before. There is some combination of heat and smell that tells me to be afraid. Once I saw my grandfather pick up a brand new toaster from Montgomery Ward and throw it at a refrigerator door. My grandmother screamed and picked up the toaster and then he threw it again, making another sunken place in the refrigerator door. Then he stayed behind the gray curtain and we didn't go to visit for six or seven Sundays in a row.

"Oh, it came down real hard around midnight," my mother is saying to my grandfather as she comes down the yard.

"Nearly two inches downtown," my grandfather says. "The bus almost didn't make it through there at Erdman Avenue."

My grandfather turns toward the Studebaker. My father is back at the engine. My grandfather walks around to the opposite fender—the one that is out in the street. "You going to speak to me?" he says, talking down toward the engine.

"What do you want?" my father says.

"Why must I want something?" my grandfather says, his voice raised.

My father sinks down deeper toward the engine. One of his feet leaves the ground as he bends over the fender. My grandfather turns away from the car and stares across the street toward the cove.

"How about a walk, Edwin?" my grandfather says.

"I've got the brakes to do yet," my father says.

"You need help?"

"Mr. Jackson across the street usually helps."

When my father is finished with the engine he gets the jack out and starts to jack up the front wheel nearest the sidewalk. I watch the car move up into the air and wonder why the wheel stays on the ground so long. When the car is up at an odd high angle, my father slides a red metal stand under it. When he jacks up the other wheel, my grandfather slides another stand under the other side of the car. They do not talk to each other while they do these things. My mother finishes her laundry and goes back into the house. A big cloud makes the sun go away for a time, and then my father starts to take one of the wheels apart. My grandfather squats next to the work.

"What do you want?" my father says again. "Just tell me what it is you want."

My grandfather stands and puts his hands on his hips. "Three hundred dollars," he says, almost in a shout. "I need three hundred dollars."

My father takes his hand away from the wheel and looks down at the ground. He holds a long shiny wrench, and it glints in the sun as he lets his hand fall.

"I had to give up the violin last night," my grandfather says.

"*Had* to?" my father says as he stands up. His voice is high and loud.

"I can get it back." My grandfather reaches into his back pocket and then holds out a piece of paper.

"*Gott im Himmel,*" my father says in a hissing voice, and throws the long wrench onto the street next to the car. The wrench makes a loud ringing noise as it hits the street, and when it bounces up it hits the headlight nearest the sidewalk, breaking the glass. My father looks at the headlight for a second and then picks up the wrench. "It's worth ten times that," he shouts.

"Not quite," my grandfather says.

The loud noise and the broken glass and the shouting make me begin to cry. I get off the tricycle and turn to look for my mother to come outside and make everybody be quiet.

"It's been in your family for almost a hundred years," my father is shouting now. "You've drunk away your livelihood."

"Do not shout at me," my grandfather shouts back. "I came to ask you for three hundred dollars. And that is all."

My father begins to shout again and then they are both shouting in a long string of German words that I do not understand. The words are harsh and scraping, coming from their throats and teeth, and then forced out of their mouths at each other. My mother opens the door and runs to me. She picks me up and carries me back to the house.

"You lie down for a while and then we'll have lunch," she says. I have had to go back to naps since I was hit in the head.

In the bedroom, I lie down until my mother is gone, and then stand in the bed and strain to see out the window, to watch my father and grandfather. They are still shouting at each other. Across the street, Mr. Jackson is standing on his porch with his arms folded across his chest. And Mr. Parsons is leaning on a shovel next to his house, looking across the street.

My mother picks me up from behind. I cry because I did not see her coming. She carries me with one arm around my waist, at an angle on her hip. I cry loudly as she carries me out of the house and past the car and across the street. We go down through the Jacksons' yard toward the cove. My mother does not say anything to Mr. Jackson or Mr. Parsons as we go. At the cove she puts me down and we walk out onto the Jacksons' new pier. It is the biggest one in the cove. The planks of wood are new and clean, and smell like wood. The nail heads catch the sunlight. At the end of the pier, we sit down and let our feet dangle above the water while my crying goes away completely. My mother puts her hand on the back of my neck. "We'll just stay here awhile," she says. She is crying. I can still hear the voices at the car, but they are far away. The sun is bright now, and shines down into the water to show sunfish moving in quick swirls below our feet. We sit for a long time on the pier and my mother does not say anything else. We watch the water and the fish and our own feet.

After a while, my mother says her legs are going to sleep, and we stand up. The voices are quiet. She says it's time for lunch. We walk back off the pier and through the Jacksons' yard. My father is under the Studebaker, with the bottoms of his shoes sticking out into the street. My grandfather is sitting in the car, with the door open and one leg hanging out.

"Okay, pump," my father says as we are crossing the street. And then, "hold it." When we are at the kitchen door, he says "pump it" again.

For lunch, my mother breaks saltines onto a plate and pours a mixture of tomato soup and melted cheese over them. My father and grandfather do not come in for lunch. My mother sits across from me, eating slowly and turning pages in a magazine. The kitchen gets dark as the clouds move outside. Then my mother spoons out a little dish of the orange-banana sherbet she gives me only on special occasions. When I am finished eating I go to the window to look at the sky and the car. My father is looking up the street the same way he was when I saw my grandfather coming. I go outside to my tricycle and move it up next to my father to watch my grandfather walk up to wait for the bus. As I sit on the tricycle in the wind, I do not know that my grandfather has the three hundred dollars in his pocket, or that he will live for only four more months. I do not know that the two men fighting in the street will become the basis for a whole body of neighborhood folklore about my father, or that my own memories of my grandfather will be forever entwined with the three hundred dollars, the broken headlight and the lost violin. I do know that my grandfather looks very tiny and old as he goes up the street, and that when my father goes into the house to talk to my mother, I will stand high on the pedals of the tricycle and imitate the sound of those rough foreign words.

Concussions

This is my mother, in 1952, standing at the edge of Oak Drive, leaning against one of the Armstrongs' twin Buicks. Ink-black, the Buicks are, with chrome portal trim and bumpers like liquid silver under the perfect blue sky. She is small and a sort of perfect opposite to the cars, dressed as lightly delicate as the spring itself, in mid-calf sand-colored slacks and a faded, sleeveless blouse that once had a yellow-green flower pattern to it. If you saw her from a block up the street and didn't know her, you could take her for a girl of thirteen instead of a mother of two, soon to turn thirty. The Armstrongs live across Oak and two houses up from us, and my mother is talking to Molly Armstrong about the trip my parents will begin in two days.

"Oh, Grace, he's such a good boy," Molly Armstrong says. She is big and long-boned like all the Armstrongs, who move on a large slow scale, like tractors maybe, or sea turtles. "He's never been any trouble to anyone ever, has he?"

"I guess not," my mother says. She is wistful, worried there in the sun. They are talking about me. I am six, across the street in the house, and small and shy, like everyone in our family. If the Armstongs, those many years ago, were the big range animals of the neighborhood, then we Hardins must have been the squirrels, or the monkeys—quick and nearly furtive where the Armstrongs were slow and close to lumbering, walking into every situation as if it could not unfold fully without them.

While my mother and Molly are talking, you can hear a loud, strong pounding noise from down behind the Armstrongs' house. It is Jock Armstrong, standing in the little cove of the upper bay that defines the neighborhood for its children. Every day at low tide, these days, he walks out into the water and mud in his dark green hip boots, carrying a mammoth sledge hammer to pound in the pilings that will support the pier he is building, day by day, low tide by low tide. He could be Paul Bunyan standing out there where the water will be six feet deep in a few hours, crashing his big hammer onto a wooden post with a sound like a cannon.

My mother has never been away from me for more than a few hours, and now, the day after tomorrow, she and my father will take the train to Canada to ride bicycles for two weeks, leading a group of teenagers more than seven hundred miles through parts of three provinces. "Think of it," I have heard my father tell my mother again and again over the weeks before this day. "They pay us, we get to see Canada and we get to ride the bicycles."

My little sister Lisa and I will not stay the nights with the Armstrongs but with Granna Gaither, who lives directly across Oak from us and takes care of two children each day while both their parents work. But I will spend most of the days with Molly's children. The younger two are eight and, strangely, twins. The girl is named Leamie, and is already taller than my mother, with blond hair halfway down her back. Her brother is named Garrett, and he looks more like his father than anyone his age possibly could look like a father, with the same dark, softly curling hair and shoulders too wide for his body.

The older boy is twelve, and named Trenton. Named, my father joked once with my mother, after the city in New Jersey even though the Armstrongs are originally from Pennsylvania. Jock Armstrong, big as one of his Buicks, moved his family to the neighborhood when the aircraft plants were built and he learned of the thousands of jobs that were to be had, the same way my father did. The whole neighborhood is built of people who came to work for the aircraft company and moved into the houses the company built to accommodate their families around the time of World War II. Now, Edwin and Jock are among the few in the neighborhood who no longer work there; Jock works for the big tool company in toward Baltimore, and Edwin drives a truck out in the northern part of the county, keeping watch for forest fires.

I do not know, on this day of the final arrangements, even when I come to the window to look out at her, that my mother carries two contrasting views in relation to the Armstrongs. They lend my parents tools and time, and bring gifts of food and flowers from the yard, leaving my mother with the knowledge that they are as nice and as kind as the people in the town where she grew up, down in the mountains of Virginia. At the same time there is some other feeling that she can never fully dismiss—a feeling that might have been visible on that day to an expert in body language, say, who could have seen her next to the Buicks, watched the curl of her arms around herself now and again and the turning of her head to one side, and had a sense of her fighting her wariness built perhaps around the Armstrongs' size and northernness, or something else that she did not fully grasp; who might have surmised that her leaving Lisa and me behind had brought new magnitude to something that lived in a distant corner of her, like a worry about a disease that runs in a family, maybe, or a hurricane far out at sea.

But in these high-skied, happy days when the war is over and people have new children and new cars and new washing machines, the families on Victory Cape are friendly and helpful to one another in a huge, American and genuine way, as if the great fortune that has been earned by their country has spread over them a coating of gratitude that needs to be shared regularly, nearly as if the thoughts my mother had back then could not exist. People stand outside beside cars as they wash them, or in the fall beside piles of burning leaves, and talk to each other—about their families, their new purchases, the Martin Company, the new beach club. And so it is that the families in the houses nearest to us on Oak have clustered around us. Not just because of that sense of neighborhood, but also because of both simple, kind interest and because of the strangeness of the coming event. No other grownups ride bicycles, and certainly no one has ever gone off to Canada without their children, or with their children either.

Trenton Armstrong is standing by the tiny cove of the bay that reaches into the far end of his family's yard, where the nail heads of Jock Armstrong's new pier catch the sunlight like diamonds. Trenton is back away from the pier, next to the remains of a pile of limestone gravel that was used to create a small boat launch between the Armstrongs' pier and the next one out toward the larger water. Trenton holds a baseball bat in his left hand—pointing it straight up at the sky without any effort—and reaches down to pick up one walnut-size rock at a time, push it lightly out of his palm into the air in front of him, move his right hand to the bat to join the left and then bring the bat through the path of the falling rock to drive it far out over the water. The noise as he hits each rock is what I think a gun must sound like, but I am even more entranced with Trenton's motions and the arcing flight of the struck rocks than I am with the big hard noise. I want to hold the bat so much that I can feel it in my hands up to my elbows and shoulders and into my eyes. The beautiful blond wood rips through the air, cracks at each rock and continues on around to bounce gently off Trenton's bare back. He pauses to look at the big part of the bat every few swings, as if the pock marks he is creating please him. I want to be able to make the same sharp, heroic collisions that he does again and again while his little brother and I watch.

"Let me try," Garrett says to his brother after we have stood and watched for a long time as the rocks fly more than halfway across the cove toward the strange flat-roofed houses on the other side.

"Get out of the way," Trenton says back, and swishes the bat lightly in the direction of Garrett, who is already far away and moves even farther back.

"He could hit a house over there if he wanted," Garrett says softly to me, as if to deflect his big brother's refusal to let him have a try.

Trenton Armstrong is the full embodiment of what I want to be. He is a boy, the same as I am, but he is completely different. His arms are tan and long and muscly, and have hair on them. His back is wide as a man's but smooth and hairless. He spends every day roving slowly around in the ends of the yards down by the cove, moving things, hitting things, throwing things. Sometimes he fishes, with a flyrod instead of the bobber lines we use—going after bass instead of sunfish. Sometimes he throws the football to us, or more often, way over our heads as he sends us out for long passes. Or he takes the rowboat out onto the cove and shouts back at us to go find something to do for ourselves. Always, he is slightly angry and unpredictable. We know he will let us do things with him—I have never seen him play with anyone his own age—but we know too that at any moment he can turn against us and tell us to get lost.

When he is tired of hitting rocks, Trenton walks up a little ways toward the garage that is down from the house next to Granna Gaither's. Up above the door there is a wicker basket—like a trash can—with a hole in the bottom that we use as a basketball hoop, and for a few minutes Trenton takes on Garrett and me, waving a purple, too-bouncy ball over our heads before he turns and arcs a big hook shot far above us. He beats us 10-3 and then slings the ball off to the side of the garage.

It is when we turn away from basketball and walk into the garage that the day changes slightly for Garrett and me—from being a part of the edges of stuff that Trenton is doing to being a full ally with him. It is nearly dark in the garage. There are no windows, and since we sort of edged our way in once we saw the door was open, we pull it almost all the way shut behind us. There are tires and other car parts inside, and an old bicycle. We pick things up and talk about them—all three of us describing what we've found at the same time, as if we're the same age, or all friends. Trenton seems pleased with the things we tell him about. He explains a tire iron to us, and the shape of a coal shovel.

In the far corner of the garage Garrett pulls out a

dusty leather bag that clanks with a metal noise as he brings it into the shaft of light. Trenton comes to it immediately and I follow. Trenton takes hold of the bag and pulls at the strap at the top to look inside. I do not know what the sticks inside are, but Garrett and Trenton are both talking about golf, and walking toward the door to take the bag and its contents back out into the day. Inside the big bag is a smaller bag, and it in are small white balls with tiny indentations in them. I have never seen this kind of ball before—so small, so hard, so white. The ball is hard as a rock and so, to see if it will bounce at all, I take it outside and throw it as hard as I can against the concrete at my feet. Before I can think or see anything, the ball comes back up and hits me in the forehead. I feel myself turn away at the same time I feel tears beginning to come. But I know what Trenton thinks about it when Garrett or I cry and so I rub hard at my eyes and forehead and say I am okay.

"Golf balls fly farther than baseballs," Trenton says. "You can hit one with a bat and it will go across the cove and over the houses over there." He comes over to me and pulls my hands away from my eyes and head, looking at my face. He laughs. "Well, no shiner, I don't guess, but you're going to have a real nice goose egg on your forehead in a couple of minutes." He laughs again, and Garrett and I do too. I don't know what a goose egg is on your head, but I can already feel the round of the swelling.

I think that Trenton is going to go find the bat and hit the golf balls across the cove, but instead he carries them just onto the grass next to the garage. He looks out in front of himself for a moment, over the long open back yards of the houses—like his—that are lucky enough to be on the side of Oak where the cove is. Then he reaches in the bag and takes out one of the golf clubs. I am surprised that it has an end on it the size of Jock Armstrong's fist, instead of a little flat-faced surface that is my image of a golf club. Trenton swings the club around him a few times the same way he does with a baseball bat, as if he is loosening up. Then he dumps the bag of golf balls out onto the ground next to him, like a cluster of Easter eggs somebody forgot to hide better in the grass. He reaches down, letting one leg come out straight behind him, picks up one of the balls and sets it on a little clump of grass. I edge up a little closer to watch, thinking about how the ball bounced onto my forehead and how far Trenton is going to hit it. I do not quite fully see the first golf back swing that I would have ever seen, because, after he has settled his hands and wriggled his hips and legs slightly, Trenton is able to bring the club back only about a third of the way it would have risen behind him before it collides, with a terrible noise that I do not hear, with my left temple just behind the eye.

My father is standing in the kitchen next to a dull-metal colored container the size of a trash can. The can is discolored on the outside with brownish bits of wax, and with thin lines of honey that have run down it to make the floor around it so sticky that your shoe makes a noise when you walk there. Around the big can in the kitchen are on-end frames from beehives, some with their comb still swelled-out with honey and others with their honey already flung out by the motions my father undertakes with the can.
    My mother does not like the extractor, because it takes up most of the room in the kitchen and creates a strange, waxy-sweet smell all through the house. Once she talked to Jock Armstrong about the honey equipment going into one corner of his tool shed instead of in her kitchen.

Jock Armstrong said that would be fine, but my father has never moved anything over there. Now, he is looking down toward the floor at dozens of envelopes all around him. The envelopes were on the counter next to the sink—left there after my father used the scissors to cut the stamps off their corners and then put the stamps into water in the sink to soak off for his collections. Before she picked up the envelopes and flung them toward my father, my mother yelled that she was tired of not having any of the kitchen for a kitchen, that she didn't want it to be a honey extraction room any longer. The envelopes started into the air as one cluster and then fluttered apart to settle onto the sticky floor around my father's feet.

It is September now, and I have started back to school. They told me in the summer that I would probably not start school on time—because of the double vision I had since the day they took the bandages off my head, a week after I woke up from the golf club accident. People said that the sort of lucky part was that I did not wake up until the day after my mother came back from Canada, three days after the accident. My father stayed there, because there was no one else to lead the trip. After the bandages were gone, I sat in the bed in the hospital and looked out the window to watch the cars— far across the hospital lawn—to try to see my mother's car. I knew the shape of a red Studebaker Champion convertible, but it was hard to be sure that's what it was when I saw two of everything, overlapping about halfway. My mother came to see me every day and stayed a long time. There were two of her too, but with less overlap than the cars.

My injuries, I would not learn until many years later, were so severe that several doctors spent several hours picking tiny pieces of shattered skull bone out of the surface of my brain. There was pessimism about my living at all and what would remain of my brain function if I did wake up. I knew nothing more of that—when I did awaken and could see again—than I did of what no one else saw either, back then, as the concurrent blow to my parents' marriage. So sharp was my mother's guilt and anger and shame over the injury to her son when she was away that she seemed, at least to my father, to forget that she had agreed to go in the first place. And so it was that the great optimism they had held together—over their trip, over the prospect of looking for another place to live—to help make room for their third child—began to become tangled in the overwhelming logistics of their lives as related to a severely injured boy, to the honey season and to the coming, in two months, of another baby.

People came to see me every day when I came home from the hospital. They brought food in casserole dishes and a Davy Crockett hat and baseball cards. The neighborhood closed over our house for a few weeks in the manner of skin growing quickly and from all sides over a wound. From the outside you could see a parade to our house, most any day, of help and health. I was not alone, at age six, in being unable to gauge what was occurring inside a house that was beginning a process of being overcome by my father's interests and hobbies. No one knew that his bee frames, his stacks of magazines and newspapers, his soaked, to-be-soaked and soaked-and-to-be-mounted stamps were squeezing my parents into undertaking the motions of their lives in different parts of the house—my father often retreating to pull his big speakers in close to him so that he could hear Beethoven or Bach and nothing of us, and my mother often taking us out of the house for walks. My parents did not see, for perhaps longer than a year, that the balm the neighborhood had worked to spread upon them—the visits and casseroles, the offers for help with the children—did not serve to heal the wound they'd suffered concurrent with mine, and that they did not realize at first had been there at all, so close upon them were the immediacies of their lives.

In fact, over the years while I grew up, while the half-dollar-size hole in the side of my head slowly closed over with new bone, the opposite was occurring, perhaps at a parallel rate, with the distance between my parents. My father's tendency to collect and save became more acute, despite my mother's intermittent efforts and admonitions to change him or at least contain the fruits of his obsessions. My friends, when they came by to get me to go to the ball field, were reluctant to come inside the house at all. There was some combination of the loud music and a father who would ask you, for instance, what books you were reading, that kept them outside. Sometimes Garrett Armstrong, brave or foolish enough to speak of it, would ask me, when we were down at the cove fishing, how I ever got to have such a crazy father. This made me think about Jock Armstrong and if he were crazy, and then I thought about not seeing him at our house for a long time.

It took the full rupture of another woman—a woman who lived only a few blocks away—for my mother to abandon her pattern of quiet retreat and optimistic parry, of staying with her children and her hobbies with fabric and soil, and to instead strike out against my father. Sometime in my teens, after she had tried and tolerated for years, she demanded her own house. My father, eaten with guilt and visited by fury of a woman scorned, bought it for her as soon as it could be arranged. And so it was that we—my mother, my sister, the brother born the summer after the accident, and the last brother—moved four blocks away to a different house.

We were, of course, the only two-house family in the little neighborhood, and our collective strangeness— spawned not only by the accident and my father's eccentricities but also our smallness, our shyness and now our two houses—became even more palpable to people. We no longer had anything much to do with any of the Armstrongs, except sometimes in the summer when the boys of Victory Cape gathered to play baseball. Trenton, by now nearly finished high school, still liked to play with us younger boys. He liked it that he could turn, with his powerful right-hand swing, on our best fast ball and drive it out over the trees at the edge of Oak and onto the street, or sometimes near a parked car or even a house across Oak. He was still as big and loud and percussive as ever, and as we played ball in those last summers while we all still lived there, neither he nor anyone else seemed to have any recollection at all that one day many years back he had raised a golf club deep into the side of my head, and that from that day onward, we Hardins had been unable to hide or overcome the realities of ourselves—to an extent that the neighborhood had grown, over those few years, to stand away from us and watch and wonder, instead of around us to help and embrace.

Sirens

I am in the third grade in the Brooker's Run Volunteer Fire Department building on the eastern side of the county. The minute hand on the big round clock behind Miss Farrington is ready to jump the last two minutes toward one o'clock. Then the second hand will arc slowly down over the two and three and four before the siren begins. Everyone except Miss Farrington is ready for the start of the siren. She is surprised every day. I watch her eyes fall at the start of the noise, and then I turn back over my shoulder to stare at Laura Baumann for the whole time the siren blares. This happens exactly the same way every day we are at school. The high noise and the smell of the heat and the sight of Laura Baumann's eyes are all crushed together into one minute that is so exquisitely loud and full that it forms the shape of the whole time I am in Miss Farrington's class.

I am from Victory Cape, where the aircraft company is. I am one of the children of the families that came originally because of the work at the aircraft plants, around the time of World War II. We are the cause of the Volunteer Fire Company building being used as a school during the year that a new school is being built. Before the aircraft company bought up the land, in the late 1920s, and for a long time after that, Victory Cape was called Harken's Point, and was indistinguishable among the many marshy peninsulas reaching out into the upper Chesapeake Bay northeast of the city. Now, in 1954, it is filled with young families who live on streets named Oak and Fir and Gum, and whose children ride tall yellow school buses to Brooker's Run. Harken's Point was renamed Victory Cape by the aircraft company during the war—at about the same time the company camouflaged all the buildings—and has been separated from the rest of the eastern part of the county because of that. The cape became a different chunk of land between the city to the south and the marshes to the north.

Laura Baumann rides a different bus to school. Hers rides over miles and miles of narrow rutted roads through the marshes. Laura Baumann lives back on Blayliss Road, where I have been only once, in a car. The road turned to dirt as it neared the water, and I saw a slunk-down Hudson Hornet up on cinder blocks, with cattails growing all around it. In my confusions over girls—over the siren and writing notes and pushing girls at recess—I have picked Laura Baumann because she is not from Victory Cape. Distaste for girls from the cape is deep and automatic, and has existed since the days when we were infants on the cape beach. Mothers spent the warm months of their twenties at the beach, cultivating tans and calling out to their children while their husbands were at work building the war. Laura Baumann is chosen because she is not part of those years, because she is apart and different, and cautious and quick-eyed, like the other children from back in the marshes.

Laura Baumann is taller than I am, and her skin is smoother and darker than the other girls' who ride the marsh bus. She writes notes with Xs on them, and folds them into tiny fat squares and gives them to me at lunch. I reply not only with Xs, but also with Os and arrows and knife blades, because I draw them well. She wears soft jumpers with designs of trains and daisies and animals on them. She carries a blue book bag and a lunch pail that has Davy Crockett on the outside and occasionally a cookie for me on the inside. She brings these things from back on Blayliss Road, where I picture her living in one of the low, flat-roofed houses that I remember seeing by the water. There is a feel of raw, rural energy in my vision of the place where she lives, and that energy is in her eyes when I look through the siren noise at her while Miss Farrington bows her head.

In the sixth grade there are new styles of romance. Notes and stares remain, as do initials on notebooks, but by now there is a group of four girls, including one from Victory Cape, and a corresponding number of boys, who trade partners every few months, as if with the seasons. We are all in the Baygreen Elementary School, just a few miles from Victory Cape. Behind the school is a grove of trees, and in April of the sixth grade, my friend Thackery Malcom and I have convinced two of the girls to walk down there after school. Thack and I are now old enough to skip the bus and walk home if we want to. One of the girls lives near the school and is part of the group that at the transportation assembly is called the walkers. The other girl is Laura Baumann, who is still at school because she waits, on some afternoons, for her mother to pick her up. Thack's girlfriend is Laura Baumann and mine is the walker. Her name is Rosalia Maracino, and she has short dark hair and sometimes uses cuss words.

We are all four in the trees, and the girls have reverted to habits from earlier grades. Thack and I are holding their hands, but they are pulling away to be able to whisper at each other. They are talking about getting home before their mothers miss them. But under two tall poplar trees that shade the cove, Thack kisses Laura Baumann and I kiss Rosalia. I think I am doing well because the noise sounds like kissing to me. But at the other poplar, Thack and Laura are holding their mouths together without breathing, which seems both impossible and foolish to me.

On a Friday in May we are in the woods with the girls and Thack is reaching with a stick to retrieve a floating bottle and Rosalia is watching him. Laura Baumann and I are leaning against one of the kissing poplars. Without thinking I lean toward her and we begin to kiss, long and quiet, without breathing. Thack turns and sees us, and then Thack and I fight in the mud at the edge of the cove. There is mud on his eyes, and I can taste the salt in the water. He tears my shirt collar all the way off and throws it out into the cove. I have a knot on my head where I hit it on a root. Thack is only wet and muddy when we stop fighting. I want to reach out and tear his shirt so we will be even, but I am afraid of being down in the mud again. The girls are gone. Thack and I walk home together, at first threatening to fight again, and then talking about starting a club of just guys who have been in real fights. This is the first real fight for both of us, and after a few days we decide to trade girls for the woods the next Friday.

In June, I am with Laura and Thack and Rosalia near the cove. We are talking about what will happen next year when we might be going to different junior high schools. The time is far away, but we are grim over the possibilities. Thack tells Rosalia that he will go wherever she goes, and takes her hand to walk along the shore. There is a breeze in the poplar leaves and a big white cloud above the school. I look into Laura Baumann's eyes and remember all the way back to the third grade and the siren. I am as held by love as someone nearly twelve can be. I hold her by the shoulders and tell her that I will meet her here over the summer.

"Oh no," she says immediately. "The buses won't be running."

I look at the ground, considering her point.

"Besides, it's too far," she says, building her case.

"My bike," I say. "I could ride my bike over here and meet you at the school."

"But how would I get there?"

I am stumped again. I decide that Laura Baumann does not want to see me after school is over. This makes me feel all the more certain that I cannot survive the summer without seeing her. "I could ride right to your house," I say finally.

"But you don't know where I live."

In the end Laura Baumann gives me detailed directions to her house, using gas stations and churches as landmarks, and telling me how to avoid having her mother see me. I feel Laura and I are again on the same side. I watch her eyes as she tells me, and then I kiss her. I tell her I will be there the day after school is over. The woods are warm with the promise of summertime. But those months, which open with a burst of heat, belong to baseball and fishing and turtle hunting, and I do not miss Laura Baumann until it is time to go back to school.

It is late in the seventh grade. I have not seen much of Laura Baumann, though we are in the same school. She is in 7-G and I am in 7-L. Thack has convinced me to go to a dance. He has been talking about how Karen Fisher will let you put your hand on her bra when no one else is around, and so I have come to the dance. I have made no progress since kissing in the woods, and have begun to feel I am being left behind.

The dance is in the gymnasium. Mr. Perkins is sitting near the stage at a cafeteria table with a record player on it. He is still wearing his phys-ed teacher clothes. The air is warm and thick in the gym. I stand next to Mr. Perkins at the table and watch people dance. Mr. Perkins asks me if I want to pick out some records. I take a stack of records in one hand and hook the good ones over the thumb on my other hand. I feel important standing there in front next to Mr. Perkins, picking out records.

Mr. Perkins plays "All I Have To Do Is Dream" first. It is my favorite song, and I look around to see who will notice that I have picked it out. Then I see Laura Baumann, dancing near Mr. Perkins' table. She is dancing with a tall thin boy that I have never seen. He is wearing a short-sleeved shirt with the sleeves rolled up, and his hair is combed straight back. Laura's face is pressed up against his shoulder and her arms are draped around his back. The boy's neck is bent down so that his face is pressed into Laura's hair. They are very close to each other and are hardly moving at all while the Everly Brothers sing my favorite song. I leave the dance and walk all the way home by myself, throwing my clip-on tie into the ditch next to Bay Drive. I decide that I will never go to another dance.

For the rest of the seventh grade, I look for Laura Baumann in the hall. I need to meet her eyes, to show her with my stare what a terrible thing she has done to me. But when I do see her, I turn away, unable to look into her eyes. I have been cheated. I cannot go to dances, and Laura Baumann can. And Thack comes home from the dances and tells me things that Laura Baumann does in the parking lot after the dance is over. I want to hit Thack, but I do not.

By the time we are in the first year of high school, I have become relatively immune to Laura Baumann. I see her in a group of loudly dressed and overly made-up girls outside the school. It is fall, and I am getting ready to start a cross country workout. The girls are walking in a close pack, some with blue notebooks pressed against their breasts, and all with big purses hanging from their shoulders. They are talking about a girl, not among them, who is quitting school to marry a boy who plays in a band. Laura Baumann is no longer taller than I am. She wears a straight green skirt, above her knees, and loafers without socks or stockings. Her hair is combed high, and there are spots of acne medication on the soft parts of her cheeks. Her laugh is sharp. It cuts through me as a reminder that she has moved on and I am still stuck at kisses in the woods in elementary school. It is as if I am invisible to the whole group as they talk about the girl who is going to marry the boy in the band. The boys they are aware of are in uniforms or cars. This boy in the track shorts, though they know his name, is still a child. I have not spoken to Laura Baumann for perhaps three years. It is as though she has decided to forget who I am. I am at last taller, but she is still somehow far ahead of me. Her world is already built around people getting married and buying cars; mine is still defined by the number of boys who can run faster than I can, and the number who cannot.

After I have been away from Victory Cape for nearly twenty years, I visit my brother over a series of several summers. He has remained all his life in the neighborhood where we grew up, and lives in one of the original houses built by the aircraft company in the 1940s, when our parents moved to Victory Cape. The houses, which many doubted would last for twenty-five years, are still sound, and sell for fifteen or twenty times their original purchase prices. Nearly all have been expanded. The water around the cape, after years of steadily worsening pollution, is beginning to come back. Brian owns a twelve-foot outboard, and I take several long, slow trips around the points of land that framed my childhood. My first explorations on the visits were by bicycle, but they were discouraging. The wild, narrow roads through the marshes had been transformed into wide, lined highways leading to so many new apartment complexes, all with names emphasizing their nearness to the water. Bay's Edge Estates. Harbour Village. Shaded Cove Apartments. The aircraft company fell into decline during the late '50s and, after mergers and sales, maintains only a vestigial presence on the land. Its deep marks on the cape are nearly erased, and the growth all over the eastern part of the county has returned it to pre-war parity with the other points of land northeast of the city. The war babies from that part of the county have long since grown up and married and had children who have grown, and caused the marsh lands to become covered with apartments. My brother's new quadrangle map from the Geological Survey shows large, unnatural-looking purple areas where the marshes used to be. "Purple tint indicates extension of urban areas," says the note at the bottom.

And so it is only from the water that the land still appears to be mostly trees. I take the boat into the shallow coves and swampy river mouths to find the one that will return me for an instant to my childhood. Out in the boat I can remember the snaky rutted roads and the sense of dangerous remoteness that used to exist on the land before I grew up and moved away. It is on one of these boat trips that I see Laura Baumann for the first time since our senior year in high school. I am out on a Saturday, in spite of threatening weather. When, in the early afternoon, the wind increases and the sky darkens, I seek shelter at the head of a small cove. I cut the motor and allow the boat to drift into the muddy shore. I see no houses, and decide to walk, to explore this section of land that still looks innocent while I wait out the weather. I have walked only a short distance when the wind calms and a light rain begins to fall. Soon I see a deeper cove, hidden from the point where I left the boat. As I come around the point, I see two people on a dock at the far end of the larger cove. They are fishing.

I walk slowly along the shore, and as I draw closer to the dock, I decide to admire the couple because they have not let the rain chase them away. Still they seem not to have heard me. Near the dock, facing their backs, I decide I should not interrupt after all. I turn to leave and am then discovered.

"Any trouble?" the man calls to me.

I assure him there is none, mention the boat, and begin to turn away, smiling.

"You from around here?" The voice carries more curiosity than wariness.

"Victory Cape." I start again toward the dock, as the woman turns. Her long hair straightened against her head by the rain, she is at first only familiar, and then slowly, almost surely Laura Baumann. I start slowly out onto the dock.

"You're a good ways out for a rainy day," the man says. He is my age. Taller, stronger-looking than I am, with clear eyes and high cheek bones. He is dressed in denim cut-offs and a Baltimore Orioles t-shirt. He stands slope-shouldered and relaxed.

"Oh, it's not all that far by boat," I say. Laura Baumann

sits facing the water, her bare feet swinging above it. She pivots at her waist to look at me, and smiles with a softness that neither reveals nor denies recognition. She sets her pole on the dock and stands. She wears white duck shorts that are slightly, pleasingly, dirty. They hug at her upper legs, trying to roll toward her hips. Her blouse is a man's pin-striped shirt, tied at the waist. Her face is full, on the brink of carrying too much weight. She rubs her hands up and down the legs of her shorts as she stands.

"Laura Nelson," she says to me, extending her hand and smiling. "And this is Don." Her voice and eyes have softened over the many years since high school, and seem to extend mild, casual kinship, as if she recognizes me but wants to spare us the awkwardness of trying to recall some moment that would be painless for all three. Or perhaps she recognizes me only as another who has come from this part of the land. I pronounce my name as I shake Don's hand. The rain comes slightly harder. "What are you catching?" I ask.

"Not much at all," Don says. "The water's just getting to the point where it's clean enough to support anything but catfish. This cove seems to have been one of the worst."

There is a pull against Don's line as he speaks. His foot traps the pole and then he reaches for it. As he does this, the one o'clock whistles from the fire departments all over the county begin to rise, nearly in unison, with the sound of dogs just behind. For a moment I am puzzled or embarrassed as I meet Laura Nelson's glance within the noise. On the dock in the rain, the whole eastern part of the county is gathered around us by the sirens. Days and years and peninsulas are drawn together. This sound runs quietly and thinly through us with the invisibility and strength of catgut line, connecting us faintly to each day we have lived. Don has caught a large white perch. He is smiling and talking as the sirens fade. I congratulate him on his catch and wish Laura luck, gesturing toward her pole. Hands are raised to accompany brief words of departure. As I walk back to the boat, the rain is steady and warm in my face, and the silence after the sirens is filled with the high faint ring of rain on water.

Dirt

When the addition to the house was completed, there was a big hill of red-orange dirt left in the back yard. The bulldozer had scraped it up into a pile around the sweetgum tree at the back edge of the yard before the construction began. The surface of the hill turned to mud in the rain and then cracked open in dry spells, and at several spots dandelions and other weeds worked to establish it as a permanent part of the yard. I had paid no particular attention to the hill, except on several occasions in the winter when the snow covered it completely enough that it appeared to be a big drift. But in the spring when I turned eleven, my father took me outside on a Saturday morning to talk about the dirt and the slow choking of the sweetgum. Then we walked across Oak Drive and on down behind the Armstrongs' house to the cove.

"Mr. Armstrong is worried about erosion here at the base of his pier," my father said, squatting to point at land which was torn into long cracks that paralleled the shoreline just beyond. "And he is quite willing to have our dirt moved over here to help save his land." My father ran a hand over a big division in the earth. I looked down at the back of my father's head. The hair was almost completely gone, and a flat spot of scalp shone in the sun. I knew what was to come. I was to be called upon to be mature beyond my years, which was my reputation within the family, and my father's favorite tool for managing me.

"And he says we're welcome to use his wheelbarrow to get it over here." My father stood then, and started back up into the Armstrongs' yard. "The route he figures we should use will come right along the hedge here, and down the yard to the cove." I looked at the hedge, feeling the trap close, and affected a pained face.

"Your mother and I put a lot of effort into the addition," my father went on, as if beginning a rehearsed response for the unhappy face. "Not to mention time and money, and we feel it's time that you take some responsibility too."

"So I have to bring the dirt over, right?" I had become impatient with the time it was taking him to actually assign the work.

"That's what we had in mind," my father said. He pulled a folded piece of paper from his back pocket. It showed a calendar, with some of the days having pencilled Xs through them. "Until school is out you won't have to do any during the week. But you'll be expected to take seven loads a day on Saturday and Sunday. And then, when school is out, you can do seven on every day until the hill is gone."

"What do I get paid?" I said, fending off more mature questions.

"Paid?"

"Yes, I think I should either get paid by the load or get a big raise in my allowance."

"Well, now, Alex, this is to be your part of the building

of the addition that we all live in. You are getting older and stronger, and can accept more responsibility as a part of the family."

I was stalled momentarily by the mention that I was getting stronger. "But I have to do it for free? Seven loads all the way to the cove for free? That's a long way." My father looked along the Armstrongs' hedge and then down to the water. "I'll talk to your mother," he said finally, and then took me down into Mr. Armstrong's basement to show me where the wheelbarrow would be kept.

The news of the seven-loads-a-day edict spread quickly among my friends. Their reactions, predictably open-mouthed, provided me with perspective on the degree of cruelty being inflicted. Other fathers went too far from time to time, but this was the worst yet. With strengths brought on by peer urgings and logical reasoning, I negotiated with my mother a doubling of my allowance and a release from Sunday work. I used Sunday School, to now my most hated responsibility, as a bargaining tool. Reverend Weathers of course discouraged hard work on Sundays.

But even with the successful negotiations, the world was unduly disturbed by the intrusion of the wheelbarrow into Saturday. Life was framed around baseball—playing every afternoon after school and listening to the Orioles games on the radio. On Saturdays I cleaned my room and then, if there wasn't a game at the field, spent the afternoon moving the radio dial back and forth between Oriole at bats and the new Top Forty, rooting equally hard for the home team and my favorite song to move up in the standings.

When school was out for the summer, the burden became more regular. The sense of dread that had surrounded only Saturday now engulfed the whole week. I played ball every day at the field, and left my loads until late in the day. I quit one evening after my third load turned over in the middle of Oak Drive. My father came running out of the house, shouting at me to be more careful. He helped me get the dirt up off the street, but there was a big orange circle left in the street between our house and the Armstrongs'. I asked for a meeting with both of my parents. I sat down at the kitchen table, the sweat running down my bare chest.

"Seven is too much," I said. "I've spilled at least ten loads so far, and my arms are sore and I've got blisters." I had been out of school four days and had spilled three loads.

"Don't fill it so full," my father said.

"Then it'll take forever to get finished," I said, and hit the kitchen table.

My mother suggested five loads a day.

"Five?" My father's voice was high and incredulous. "Then he *will* never get it done."

I put my face on the table, showing them the top of my head. In the end it was decided that I would do six, but would have to get them finished before I played ball or went fishing or did anything else. And I would have the whole weekend off. I was not fully satisfied with the compromise, but I got up from the table and went into my room to cross off the days I wouldn't have to work after all.

Half the infield, the catcher and an outfielder had to pass the house to get to the ball field, and they stopped the next morning when they saw me out by the tree shoveling dirt into Mr. Parsons' wheelbarrow. I was usually first at the field.

"Come on," said the catcher. "Check the new Harvey Kueen bat I got last night." He cradled the bat for me to see.

I threw the shovel onto the dirt hill and told them about the new rules. I kicked dirt chunks as I spoke.

"Geez," the third baseman said, "your father really went overboard on this one." My father had once chased the third baseman out of the house for humming the "Bonanza" theme while he was listening to a Mozart record. And another time for accidentally putting a big rip in a page of a big magazine called *Show*, to which my father was proud of being a charter subscriber. The third baseman stayed clear of my father. I picked up my shovel and pushed it, with some sighing ceremony, into the dirt.

"You got another shovel?" the outfielder said.

"Two more in there," I said, pointing at the storage space at the back of the house. "But you guys don't need to stay here."

"We'll get six loads out in no time with all five of us," the outfielder said. He went to get the shovels and came back with a pickaxe too. So, with one to loosen and three to shovel, the six loads were done quickly. I began to think about getting ahead on my days. With the help, I could get ten or twelve loads done in one day, and then take a day off.

When my father came home that evening, I showed him the calendar with the extra day marked off. I had come home after baseball and done my own six.

"Grace, is this correct?" my father called out to the kitchen.

"Yes, it is," she said. "Alex got some help from his friends today. They all worked very hard. They wanted him to be able to play ball."

My father did not react well to this, for a reason that I could not understand, and when they finished talking, my father went into the living room to watch the news. He got upset over something having to do with the president and then put on some loud classical music. I went into my room and listened to the Orioles. They lost to the Indians.

As the summer wore on and the dirt pile at last became perceptibly smaller, my friends helped less and less. The day-long baseball games became less regular, as the leagues had started by now, and everyone got to play twice a week, with lettered t-shirts and hats and a real umpire. The summer had begun to stretch out into long hot days, though there was still enough left that no one had begun to talk about going back to school. I knew I had gotten stronger from moving all that dirt, and sometimes after supper when I went down to the cove to fish, I sat and admired the thick hard calluses across the palms of my hands. But I hated the dirt, and the thought of my father checking the paper every night when he came home from work.

In late August there was a day when I went on strike. The volunteer fire department was setting up the carnival in the morning, and I had received explicit orders to get the loads done before I went up to the big field around the fire hall to help set up. You could see the field from the edge of the cove, and on my third load, I got angry enough about everyone but me being there that I flipped the wheelbarrow straight over the bank so that the handles stuck down into the water. I threw a few big dirt clods at the turned-up belly of the wheelbarrow, and then took off for the carnival, where I would spend the whole day helping put up booths and spreading wood chips.

By the time I went home, my father was there. The wheelbarrow was parked out in front of the house, muddy handles pointed at me as I came into the yard. I was to clean the handles, apologize to Mr. Armstrong, eat my supper, and go to bed. Further measures were being contemplated, my father told me.

The next day was Saturday, and in the morning before the Top Forty show came on, I was sitting on the bed I had just made, reading the backs of baseball cards. The little cartoon said that Johnny Vander Meer once pitched two no-hitters in a row. There was a knock at the door. I knew it was my father, because my mother and brother and sister had already left to go to the carnival, for the whole day. I expected to be sent to the cove to finish yesterday's loads, or to be confined to my room for the weekend.

"Alex, it's been a long summer," my father said, and then paused while he found a place to sit on the bed. "And you've really worked hard with the dirt. Do you realize you're getting very close to being finished out there? You're really coming along." He paused again, and then started to talk again, using his rehearsed-sounding voice. "I'm sorry I was harsh with you yesterday. Maybe we were both wrong."

I put down my baseball cards and smiled even though I didn't quite want to. "It's okay," I said. "I shouldn't have dumped it into the cove." I felt myself start to smile again.

"And you and I haven't done anything together all summer," my father said. "I thought maybe we could do something today." My father looked down when he was finished, as if he were embarrassed.

I was surprised by the offer, and could not immediately think of anything. On the last day of carnival set-up, no kids were allowed in, and my father didn't like the carnival anyway. And the things I liked best—playing baseball, fishing, riding my bicycle over to Rosemont—were things my father did not do. We had gone hiking together once on the Appalachian Trail, covering the whole length of the trail in Maryland, when I was nine. And we had tried tennis once, but I had quit quickly.

"Anything you want," my father said into the silence.

"Well, I don't know. I can't think of anything right off." I was embarrassed by the attention being shown me, and by my father being embarrassed too.

"There's a concert in Leakin Park this afternoon," my father said finally. "Very light. Some Strauss waltzes, a little Haydn."

I felt my face wrinkle. "I don't know," I said. "I never liked your kind of music all that much."

My father stood up. "You think about it. There's a great deal more to music than you hear on that little box, with all the whining and twanging. You might enjoy it." He ran his hand over my hair. "You think about it and let me know."

When my father was out of the room, I picked up my baseball cards again, thinking about something to do. Babe Ruth held the record for most consecutive shutout innings by a pitcher in World Series history, it said on the back of a card. I read over my Orioles cards, though I knew them by heart. I went out to the living room to find my father.

"See these?" I said, holding up the cards.

"Yes," my father said slowly.

"They gave me my idea." I had tried, not long after the Orioles came to town, to get my father to go to a game. He had refused politely, and so I had moved on alone, with only an occasional attempt since, to convince my father of the perfection of the game.

"Now I don't know about that," my father said, with a face that was similar to the one I had made when I had heard about the concert in Leakin Park. "You know I don't know a thing about baseball."

"Oh, but you could learn," I said immediately, complete with my father's intonation and hand movements. "It's only fair for you to give baseball a chance if I give the concert a chance."

My father could not dispute this logic, perhaps feeling some pride that he helped instill it in his son, and so the bargain was made. The concert in Leakin Park that afternoon, and then out to Memorial Stadium that evening to see the Orioles play the Senators. I was glad that it was the Senators who were in town, because the Orioles, even in their infancy as a franchise, beat the Senators with some regularity.

During the time it took us to get ready, I imagined us at the stadium. I would explain pinch hitters and relief pitchers and tell my father about Willie Miranda, who was the Orioles' shortstop and my favorite player. The day became huge and exciting around me, and I did not remember that I would miss the new Top Forty while we were at Leakin Park. I was finally getting a chance to show baseball to my father.

At Leakin Park, my father was irritated by people walking around instead of sitting down and listening to the music. I sat on a folding chair behind a man with white hair, and tried to listen. Mostly I thought about the baseball game. My father moved his head with the music and sometimes made little *ta-ta-ta* noises to go along with it. I recognized a few of the melodies from hearing them at home. There was one I liked, and I asked my father what it was.

"That was 'The Waltz of the Blue Danube,'" my father said brightly, and smiled at me. "You liked that one?"

"It's the best so far," I said. "What's the Blue Danube?"

"The Danube is a river," my father said. "Partly in Germany. It runs through the town where your grandfather was born." My father said a long German town name. I had once been shown the town on the map by my grandfather before he died, when I was four or five. I remembered my grandfather as an old man who often was angry and who played the violin. In some vague way, I blamed my father's strictness on both he and his father having been born in Germany, where people marched around like robots.

When the concert was over, my father stood up and clapped. Some of the people were leaving while my father was standing there clapping. I sat in my seat and watched my father. It was a long time before he stopped clapping, and I could see how much he had enjoyed the music. This made me happy, for a reason that I didn't know, and suddenly I wanted to hug him for being so nice to the musicians. But I did not do it right away, and then my father stopped clapping.

In the car my father hummed some of the pieces from the concert, and told me about the place where we would eat. The place was called The Belair, and my father had not been there for a long time. He drove quickly and easily in the city traffic and talked about the concert in a way that made me feel that he was pretending I knew all about concerts. I thought about the baseball game and about how important it was for the Orioles to win, so that my father could see how good my favorite team was.

When he found out that The Belair Restaurant had been turned into a dry cleaners, my father started a long talk about the city being changed, about all the old places being torn down for parking lots and gas stations and White Coffee Pots. We went to the Marylander Cafeteria and ate turkey sandwiches and Jell-O. My father continued to talk about the city being torn down, and I could not find a place to bring up the Orioles. My father had lost all his enthusiasm for the concert over The Belair being a dry cleaning store now. He said that he and my mother had gone to The Belair years ago, even before they were married.

When we finally got to Memorial Stadium, my father was irritated with the crowd. "People just bump into you," he said, "and don't say a word."

I took us to Gate E-4 to get our tickets. My friends and I always went to E-4 and then sat out in the right field bleachers so we could yell at the opposing team's right fielder. "Don't knock the Rock," we yelled at Rocky Colavito until he turned around. "Hey Lemonhead," was what we used on Jim Lemon. We always wanted to yell at Jimmy Piersall, but he always played center field, and couldn't hear us. People said Jimmy Piersall would climb into the stands after you if he knew you were yelling at him.

When we had our seats, my father said the stadium was very big, and asked why they were watering the dirt part of the field. "Are they trying to grow grass in there?"

I kept myself from laughing and explained about good true hops on a nice infield and about water keeping the dust down. I was pleased at having explained these things to my father. My hands were wet with anticipation of the game and with the prospect of explaining more about baseball to my father.

When everyone clapped and whistled and shouted as the Orioles ran onto the field, my father looked all around him and then turned to me, looking puzzled again. "Why are they clapping?"

"For the Orioles," I said as I clapped. This seemed to be a foolish question. I fought the tears I always felt coming when I stood in a crowd of people clapping for the Orioles.

"But they didn't do anything but run onto the field," my father said, his voice going high. That's not much to cheer about, is it?"

For the first of many times that evening, I did not have

an answer for my father. The question was unfair and queer, I decided. It was as if my father did not want to understand, or wanted to understand on some completely different level. There was no answer. The team came onto the field and you clapped. You were glad to see them and you wanted them to do well. It was just something you did, like the seventh inning stretch. Next, my father wanted to know why the national anthem was played on a record instead of live. I hadn't known it was on a record. My father asked why the players chewed tobacco and spit—if their skills were somehow increased by their use of tobacco. He wanted to know why the pitcher took so long to throw the ball, and why a man couldn't at least get to first base when he hit the ball all the way to an outfielder. The questions seemed perverse to me, and taken in tandem with the score, began to irritate me. I couldn't yell at the right fielder when my father was there. I couldn't jump and whistle and shout out players' names. I told my father about Willie Miranda being from Cuba and my father wanted to know how a Cuban could be named Willie. In the sixth inning Willie Miranda made a throwing error and the Senators went ahead 6-1. I explained that the Orioles almost always beat the Senators, but my father did not seem to understand his son's need for sympathy in the face of defeat for the home team. He said he was always glad to see an underdog win.

In the end the Senators won, 8-3. I was so upset with the score and with my father's unanswerable questions that I gave up trying to defend the Orioles. We said almost nothing on the way home. In my room, I had the feeling that I hadn't really been to a baseball game. As I fell asleep I wondered how it was that my father could take such an odd approach to baseball, how he could pass up all the real meaning and excitement and worry about how they played the national anthem. I stayed unhappy all the way to Sunday afternoon, when the Orioles beat the Senators to take the series, three games to one. I thought more about the game with my father and decided it was no use to try to change his mind about baseball. I would just go ahead on my own. But I did tell my father that the Orioles won three of the four games with the Senators, and asked him if he knew about Washington.

"Well, somewhat," he said, irony in his voice.

"Washington," I told him just the way I heard it on the radio, "first in war, first in peace, and last in the American League."

By Monday things were completely back to normal. My father went back to work and I went back to my pile of dirt, which really was much smaller. And five working days later, after the carnival was gone, the end of the dirt pile kind of snuck up on me. I realized that it was nearly gone and did eight loads on the last day. I spilled the next-to-the-last one in the middle of Oak Drive when I hadn't seen a potato chip truck coming. The spill left a new orange stain not far from the one from back at the beginning of the summer, and though I cleaned it up long before my father got home, he noticed the new spill place before he noticed that the pile was completely gone.

After supper I went down to the cove to sit on the Armstrongs' pier and catch a few sunfish. The late sun cut down through the clean, shallow water to show me their small, circular movements and quick, nervous nibbles as I sat on the pier. I used only the tiniest pieces of worm to get the sunnies to bite. After a while, one of the older boys came down onto the Armstrongs' pier. He walked on past me out to the end of the pier and began to whip a long fly line above his head. The line sang in a high whine as the air began to change from orange to gray-orange. The boy threw his line again and again, letting it fall so very lightly onto the still water. The boy never looked back over his shoulder at me while I caught one sunfish after another and the fly line never even got a strike. When the sun was gone, the older boy walked past me and back off the pier and past the new bank that I had built, and on back up into the neighborhood. I could not figure out how it was that a boy who was already in high school couldn't figure out that you catch a lot more fish with a worm and a sinker than with a fly line.

When it was nearly dark and the mosquitoes had begun to sing around me, I got up from the pier. I had kept the biggest of the sunnies in the bucket, and now I let them go, one at a time. There were seven of them, and each was at least eight inches long. I dumped the water out of the bucket and put my worm can down into the bucket and then ran the casting rod through the handle of the bucket up to the reel, so that I could carry all of my fishing gear in one hand. I paused at the end of the pier to look at my calluses and at the dusky outline of the raw new land I had made. I thought about that because of me, there was a change in the neighborhood that would be there forever, and then I stepped down off the pier. I followed the path I had worn with the big front wheel of Mr. Armstrong's wheelbarrow, and tapped at the hedge with my pole as I walked. In the middle of Oak Drive I stopped to make sure my newest stain was still visible in the fading light. The street light made it appear to be a good strong reddish color. As I went up the walk to the house, I thought to myself that there would be a day in the wintertime when the snow would suddenly melt away so that everyone would be able to see the street again, and my father would come out into the sunshine and see the stain and come over to me to say something about how he remembered back in the summer, when I had freed his sweetgum.

Key Box

MORNING. This was during the summer when my mother was thirty-six and I was twelve, at the edge of dawn, when I awoke for a reason I did not know. The light was eerie and orange-gray, and I decided the strange color was because it was coming through the tent, which was the color of a pumpkin. My mother and I had put it up at the beginning of the summer, in the campground just over the big dune that protected us from the ocean. I was surprised to be awake. My sister and brother, younger than I, were asleep in their sleeping bags at one of the back corners of the big tent. But in the corner opposite at the front of the tent, my mother's bag was empty. Her cloth bag of clothes and her little toiletries container sat in the odd light next to the tent wall where they always sat, but her sleeping bag was flat on the tent floor.

I raised up on an elbow to look more carefully around the tent. The little broom and dustpan and the purple box with the Scrabble game in it sat in the other back corner where they always were. My mother had given me a corner at the front so I could help her make sure

Brian and Lisa felt protected, back away from the zipper at the front on nights when it was windy or rainy. Now I felt a need to survey, to make sure they were safe. I decided my mother must have gone to the restroom, near the center of the campground. The campground held about fifty tents and the same number of travel trailers, all set up for the whole summer. Up on my elbow, I listened intently and heard only a slight breeze at the screened openings along each side of the tent, and farther away, the faint sound of the sea. I waited what seemed long enough for my mother to come back, and then inched my way out of the sleeping bag. I moved slowly so as to make less noise, and not wake my sister and brother.

I was not sure where I was going, but headed first toward the restroom. Outside the tent, the air was cool and still orange-gray. The dirty sand of the road was cold on my feet, and I walked with my arms folded across my chest, as an older person would, taking little steps. I walked past five or six sites before I saw anyone else up. I saw an old man I did not recognize, smoking a cigarette in a lawn chair inside his mosquito netting. Through the netting in the early light, the man's face looked greenish and creased. When I saw the creased face, I thought of the little girl in the campground—Lenna was her name—who had brought a pet iguana to the beach for the summer. The iguana had escaped, and Lenna and her family had put a sign up at the concession stand with the big words LOST IGUANA at the top. The notice asked people to keep an eye out for Lenna's pet. When it rained the next day, my mother took us into Rehoboth to the library to look at pictures of iguanas. They were green and scaly and ugly, and my mother read out loud that they could occasionally get as big as a small alligator, but that they were harmless. When we got back to the campground, my mother asked Lenna how big her iguana was, and Lenna told her about a foot long. My mother told Lenna to maybe put the size on the notice by the concession stand, and that we would all watch out for it.

I walked past the biggest campsite in the campground, the one that was twice as big as the others. In the middle of it was a long silver travel trailer that gleamed so brightly in the daytime that I felt I couldn't go near it. I didn't like the trailer. It was on the only campsite where there was more than one car parked. One of the cars was a white Cadillac—a brand new 1958 El Dorado, I knew—and early in the summer, when my family had been settled in only a few days and the last of the sites were just filling up, four of the people who lived in the silver travel trailer came to visit us. They were nearly as shiny as the travel trailer and the cars.

The man was as old as my father, with a dark mustache and his t-shirt sleeves rolled up to show big tan muscles. The woman had tall blond hair, a bright orange bathing suit that fit right against her skin all over, and a tan almost as deep as my mother's. They were the mother and father, I decided, and the other two people—high school boys with arms growing to be like their father's—were the sons.

"We don't know how it happened," the blond lady had said, talking to my mother, with her arms folded right up under her big orange bosom. Before she could finish speaking, the taller of the two boys said, "yes, we do know how—*he* did it." The mother ignored this and went on to say that somehow, sometime over the past week or so, they'd lost the only keys they had for the Caddy. "We could drive another car back home and get another key," the mother said, "but it's a hundred and fifty miles or so back to Baltimore, and we do have the other cars."

"Oh, Baltimore," my mother said. "We're from there too."

"Well," the woman said, "then you know it's a pretty good drive back."

"Yes, but your car," my mother said.

The man waved his arm. "We have the other one," he said, "but we want to ask everybody in the campground to keep an eye out just in case the keys are around here somewhere."

"They are," the taller boy said, "because he just threw them down someplace in the damn sand."

"Bull," said the other boy.

I wondered if the boys' parents were going to yell at them for cussing, or if you could do that after you were in high school.

"I bet someone finds them," my mother said.

When I came back out of the restroom into the cool morning, I decided my mother might have come out while I was in, and I overcame a wish to run over the big dune to look at the ocean. I walked back to the tent and peeked in without opening the zipper again. She was not there. I decided Brian and Lisa would be safe if I took just the time needed to run over the dune and look at the ocean for a moment before I went back to guarding them. The ocean was the biggest, most amazing thing I knew, and I felt a strong need to look at it every morning, as if to see if it had remained so huge and blue.

The dune was almost as good as the ocean itself. It rose up at the back edge of the campground, white and tall and protective, the size of the biggest ocean wave ever. My brother and sister both complained every time they climbed it to get to the beach. Your feet sunk in deep with every step, and a million grains of soft white sand ran through your toes each time you pulled your foot up. When you were on top of the dune, you could look as far as you could see either way, and the dune ran along the beach, paralleling the ocean perfectly, far up from the high tide line.

 In the morning as I climbed it, the sand was not hot the way it was during the day, but neither was it as cold as the road sand. I paused at the top of the dune and looked up to the north toward Rehoboth. I felt tall up there. The beach, usually speckled with people, was empty toward Rehoboth. In the other direction, toward Ocean City, there was no one either, except for what looked like it might be a child, far down the beach. I watched the person move a few steps and then bend down, then stand again, walk a few more steps and then squat down. I walked along the top of the dune in that direction, putting my hands up to my eyes to make binoculars out of my fingers and thumbs. I walked for a distance far enough to wonder if I was going too far from the tent. I stopped walking when I recognized my mother's blue jacket and her gray sailor hat. I dropped down flat onto the sand to hide myself, as if I were playing army.

 I lay in the cool sand and watched my mother for a long time. She was moving slowly back toward where I was, but she never looked up at the dune. She kept her eyes down on the sand, sometimes swinging her foot along the sand in front of her in an arc as if to start to draw a circle around herself, or as if to move something small in front of her. And every so often she squatted down to be closer to the sand. She carried a small cloth bag that looked like the ones she had made for my brother and sister and I to put our dirty clothes in. But her bag was smaller, and all the things she dropped into it looked small from where I watched. Shells, I knew, or little pieces of glass worn smooth by the sea. At home, she had a serving tray for each of us, and the surfaces were made of the little pieces of glass she must be picking up now. I had not thought of those trays except in their function of holding food. I thought of my mother making the trays and then, still flat on the sand, I thought of the grocery bags I had filled with acorns in the fall. I had put them in my closet and kept them there. My friends' mothers had made them put theirs outside, for fear of bugs or the bottoms of the bags rotting, or because the acorns sprouted and looked ugly. But my mother seemed to have liked the acorns. She had asked me how I'd filled six whole grocery bags, where I'd found the trees to yield all those nuts, if I had anything in mind other than to keep them in the bags. She never asked me to take them outside, and as I lay on the dune, I wondered if, back at home, the bottoms of the bags had rotted, if there were potato bugs in my closet. I thought about what my mother had said about the bags. I looked down at her by the ocean, and for a moment I could make her be someone else. Not my mother, but just a person down there. Then I made her both my mother and someone other than my mother—a woman on the beach.

Twice, there in the sand, I felt the muscles in my stomach tense with the movement that would stand me up and start me on a run down to her. I could feel my bare feet speeding over the sand. It would be a great surprise for her, because I knew she would be glad to see me. "Alex," she would say, nearly singing my name with her surprise, "what in the world are you doing up?" But both times I checked myself and stayed down, deciding to leave her to her collecting. At last, when she was close enough that I could have thrown the Pluto Platter to her if I'd brought it, I moved my flattened body backwards off the top of the dune so that the woman coming toward me wouldn't see me, and then I turned and started back to the tent. I got back into my sleeping bag near Brian and Lisa to wait for her to come back to the campsite and start cooking breakfast the way she did every morning at around eight, to wait for her to be our mother again.

DAYTIME. While I watched my mother cook breakfast, I decided I was going to find out why she had gone to the beach in the early morning. I had seen her and thought of the acorns and then thought of her as Grace Hardin instead of Mom. It was Grace Hardin who was down there on the beach looking for shells, I decided. No one else was with her, there was no one to talk to or to help out, and so she must have been Grace Hardin. Or maybe, it occurred to me, she was even Grace Coggins down there, the way she was before she married my father. At home, we all lived together with my father in the house on Oak Drive. But at the beach, my mother and brother and sister and I lived without my father. He was now a school teacher the same as my mother, and had the summers off too, but he did not go to the ocean. It occurred to me that my mother had never told us why this was, and that I had never thought to ask. Edwin just didn't come out to get in the car when we left. I tried to remember back for as many summers as I could, and tried to bring to mind the picture of when we were leaving. I remembered the current summer. My father had been away with his bees when we left. I remembered the summer before, and my father was not there either, though I couldn't recall where he'd been. I couldn't remember any summers farther back. Maybe he had still been a photographer back then. Sometimes my mother and father yelled loudly at each other when they thought their children were asleep, and I wondered if that had to do with the beach, with my father not coming along. I thought about a nice woman being yelled at, and yelling herself. I wondered if I would decide to ask my mother about that, but she spoke before I finished thinking about it.

"It's going to be a beautiful day again," she said to all of us while she mixed the flour and milk for the chipped beef to go in. Lisa and Brian sat in the big red folding chairs, sunk down low so that their heads barely reached the red cloth across the back where your back is supposed to go. Both had little blankets around their shoulders and sleep still in their eyes as they anticipated their favorite breakfast. My mother fixed it almost every morning at the beach, because we all asked her to. "And the ocean is beautiful too," she went on. "Calm and blue and smooth on top."

"How do you know?" I said, looking up at her as if I had asked her about my father. My heart raced slightly.

"I went and looked," she said, and smiled at me. "While you all were still asleep."

I started to tell her I hadn't been asleep, and then decided two things quickly and without thinking about them hardly at all. First was that maybe she went down to the beach *every* morning to look for shells, and second was that I was going to find out if that was true, and if it somehow had something to do with my father. I would do this by watching her all day long to see if she did anything else that I didn't know about, anything else that made her seem like Grace Hardin or Grace Coggins instead of Mom.

I helped my mother with the breakfast dishes more than I really had to so that I could watch her, but by the time she was rubbing baby oil on her skin to get ready to go down to the ocean, I had forgotten my plan.

Then Mr. Meroulis was there next to me. He lived in an old army-looking tent behind my family's.

"Your momma has the best tan in the campground, you know," he said. He looked at my mother and her baby oil, talking to her more than to me even though he was looking at me. He was an olive-skinned man with a slight accent, and probably as old as my grandfather. I could tell that Mr. Meroulis liked my mother. He came by our campsite often to check on her and her children.

"Good calm surf today," Mr. Meroulis said to my mother. "Nice safe surf and no jelly fish. Good day for the kids." He smiled at Brian and Lisa in the red chairs.

Lisa said there was no telling about the iguana though.

"That iguana is back out in the wild forever," Mr. Meroulis said, and waved his arm in an arc out toward the low bushes that surrounded the campground. "He's in hog heaven out there."

Lisa and Brian looked at each other and smiled. "Hog heaven," Brian said.

On the beach, I stayed with my mother on the towel at the beginning, instead of running into the water right away as I usually did.

"How nice to have you visit," she said to me, rubbing more baby oil on her dark arms.

"'Visit'?" I said. It seemed an odd word for sitting on the towel with her.

"Well, staying here for a moment instead of running right in. Or are you just tired?" She smiled to let me know she was teasing. It was the same smile she always smiled—soft and small and not quite to her teeth. It was the same smile she had used when she talked to me, on the drive to the beach, about not saying something. That was the day after the school year was over, when she loaded the four of us into her two-toned '53 Ford Ranch Wagon to drive north along Route 40 away from Baltimore, and then turn south once we had crossed the top of the bay where it narrowed enough to yield to a bridge and to become the Susquehanna River. Then she aimed us down over hot, flat Delaware where they grew all the peas in the world, and on toward the sea. I sat in the front seat with her and looked at the map, verifying again and again to myself that I knew what north and south were, and being pleased that Maryland was bigger than Delaware. What my mother had told us, when we got tired or bored on the drive, was to look for things. Certain color cars, buildings we might remember from previous trips, rivers, bridges, fields of certain kinds of vegetables, letters on signs. She had something to ask about anytime she needed it to stop my brother and sister and me from being bored or disagreeable.

At a stop for gasoline soon after we could see the sand, my mother told me that when we got back in the car, she was going to ask what we should start looking out for as we got closer.

"I know you know what it is," she said. "But I'd like you to do me a favor and pretend that you don't know." She smiled at me.

"Sure," I said, understanding that I should let my brother and sister figure it out.

"And," my mother said, "don't call Lisa and Brian any names if they don't figure it out right away."

I told her yes, I would do all that. As we drove, it was hard for me not to just talk about how nice it would be to see good old Key Box Road again. We drove for miles along the sandy soil covered with its thick growth of low-slung trees and brush. Flies lived in here, I knew, and stickers and burrs that stung as unpleasantly as the insects, and when I saw that part of the land, I knew exactly what the stings felt like, and that we were close to the ocean. The highway was narrow and black and built in a perfectly straight line, with a sandy ditch running alongside, where the mosquitoes were thicker than anywhere.

My mother told us to watch for signs on the small roads that turned off the main road every few miles toward the ocean.

"You remember the name of the one we're looking for?" she asked at last, and I looked out the side window of the car as if thinking as hard as I could.

"Key Box!" Brian said immediately, as if he had been waiting, or my mother had told him the answer in secret.

"Right," she said, almost as enthusiastically. "Key Box Road. Look for Key Box Road," she said again. "Just watch for Key Box." Key Box Road was so narrow that one car had to almost stop and wait when two cars met going in the opposite direction. The road cut through the scruffy trees beyond the road ditch and opened onto the campground full of big square tents and travel trailers.

EVENING. On an evening well into August, when a few of the people had already pulled up their campsites and left for the summer, Lisa and Brian stayed back at the campsite with Mr. Meroulis while my mother and I walked down to the ocean. This was after showers and after dinner, when it was time for the coolness to come. The evening was a pinkish color, and just the right temperature. You could feel and smell the ocean in the air almost as if part of it were above you. My mother and I walked over the big dune together without saying anything. The ocean was dark blue and calm looking, its little breakers slapping softly onto the sand and rolling up just a few feet before sliding back. As soon as we got over the dune, my mother began to look down at the sand, as she always did.

"You know, there are always things to find near the ocean," she said to me. The ocean smell was even stronger. This was a sea breeze, I knew, and when you had a sea breeze, you had no mosquitoes, and there was a good smell that made me feel strong.

"Think of all the ships that have wrecked out there and left things to wash in for people to find," my mother said, looking out across the ocean toward Spain. "Hundreds and hundreds of years of ships going down into the sea."

I looked out over the ocean. "But stuff is too heavy to wash in here, isn't it?" I said.

My mother laughed softly. "Yes, mostly it is. But you never really know. You know how Key Box Road got its name?"

I said I didn't know.

"From an old box of keys they found here years and years ago. On the beach from an old ship. Nobody knew what ship or what keys they were, but back just after the war when they were getting this shore all ready for people to use, they had to clean up all kinds of stuff that had washed onto the beach for all the years that nobody much came here. And it was that old rusty box of keys that gave Key Box its name." She waved her toe in that little arc in front of her, moving sand.

"But what are you looking for, Mom?" I said.

"Me, oh," she said, sounding surprised, or embarrassed. She looked at me. "I'm looking for most anything. Shells, beach glass, washed up stuff, anything." We walked a few steps and she didn't say anything. Then she laughed a little quick laugh and talked again. "The Pluto Platters we lost in the waves last summer, a pair of sunglasses your Aunt Lee lost here two summers ago, a little hat you used to wear, Lisa's barrettes, a horseshoe crab that's alive and in one piece..." She laughed again. "Most anything, Alex, most anything."

"Why?" I said.

We were at the edge of where the sand turned from soft and white to brown and packed. "Well," she said, "it's funny that you should ask me that. Both Mr. Meroulis and that lady in the green bathing suit two tents down have asked me the same thing the last few days. And before they did, and you did, I never thought of myself as looking for anything."

"So what are you looking for?"

"Just what I told you," she said. "Just beach junk and stuff, and whatever I find. And nothing, really. It's just a great place to explore, Alex. And to learn." She walked a few steps and then stopped me by touching my shoulder. "Can you keep a secret?" she said.

I was surprised to hear her ask that. It seemed an odd question for my mother to ask, as if she were doing something she had never done, as if she were kind of cheating somehow. She reminded me of Patsy Cannaday at school, when she had told me, before anyone else, that it was her father who had wrecked a boat just off the peninsula where they lived, and then left it there.

"What about Lisa and Brian?" I said.

"With the secret?"

"Yes," I said, "why won't they know?"

"Oh, they will, Alex," my mother said, and hugged me quickly around the neck. "It's just temporary, this secret. Another day or two and we'll show everybody."

"What is it?" I said.

"You *can* keep a secret?" She smiled at me.

"Yes," I said, feigning impatience.

She leaned toward me, again seeming like a girl. "I know where the iguana's been living," she said. I could see brightness in her eyes.

"You do?" I said. "How come you haven't taken it back to Lenna?"

"Well, I can't quite catch it yet, and if we all go down there, I think it'll run away."

"Where is it?" I said.

"It's at the far edge of the campground toward Rehoboth. There's a ditch over there like the one along the main road, except maybe even deeper. Full of lots of water and insects and other stuff that iguanas love."

"And it's in there?"

"I've seen it three times, and this morning it came up to my hand," she said. "I think the next time it'll let me pick it up."

"Geez," I said. "Can I go with you to see it?"

My mother started us walking again. "Can you get up that early?"

"Yes," I said. "I know I can because I did one day back earlier in the summer. I saw you on the beach."

"In the morning?"

"Yes," I said.

"Why didn't I see you?"

I looked down. "I don't know," I said. "I wasn't sure if I was supposed to be up, or if you were supposed to just be by yourself."

She didn't say anything back to me right away, and I told her that together we could catch the iguana and return it to Lenna.

"You're right," she said. "We can."

We were almost to the ocean now. I walked down closer to the waves to let the water come up over my feet and up my legs a little, and to think about helping to rescue the iguana. My mother kept walking along where the sand changed. I splashed at the water with a movement of my foot just like the one she used on the sand. When I looked up she was a few feet down the beach from me, looking down. She had on her gray beach hat, an old white shirt that was worn thin and a pair of shorts made of old blue jeans cut off. Her legs were dark, tanner than anyone's in the campground. I stood at the water and watched her walk a ways, and I thought again about how she was not just my mother, but also a person herself, who went out in the morning looking for an iguana. She was a woman alone at the beach with her children, but not her husband. A woman who walked on the beach every morning and every evening to look for things. To look for nothing and for everything that anyone had ever lost at the beach or even from a ship in the sea. I watched her walk and then bend down to pick something up. It was almost as if she had forgotten I was there. The air was changing color toward dusk. A wave came up higher on my legs than I'd thought it would, and took my breath away for a moment. I backed up from the edge of the water to watch my mother move slowly on down the beach. I heard a noise out on the water and turned to see a fish go back into the calm surface after a leap into the air. Then I heard my mother, calling softly back toward me. She was standing at the surf's edge now, parallel to where I was in relation to the water.

"Look, Alex," she called to me. She held her hand up in the air, water dripping away from a cluster of shiny metal glistening in the day's last light. "Looks like somebody's car keys."

THE LAKE

It was cold, early in the morning, the day after Thanksgiving. My grandfather wore a tan cotton jacket and an old-man's hat almost the same color. He sat at the wheel of a 1948 Ford he had bought for himself and painted. You could look at the lime-cream color from 20 feet away and see the brush marks. He pulled at the choke and then turned the key—glancing at me with the edge of a smile and with a full squint, against Kool smoke, that looked like a wink. Once the Ford turned over, and he edged the choke back in as the engine ran more smoothly, he looked at me again, as if to tell me to learn this, or as if he were showing off, which I knew, even at age twelve, he was not. He used only his thumb and one finger at the choke, but his hand was wrapped around it full-fist. The concentration between us was strong. He was imparting something to me, I knew in a vague way, but I didn't know what it was.

My grandfather was in his fifties. His face was creased deep through the cheeks, from genes that would later do the same to my mother's face at about that age, and from the Kool cigarettes that sent smoke up into it. He was a smallish man in his jacket and cotton fedora, but sat big in the Ford, and moved big when he was outside, where we were headed. I was scrawny and as aware of myself as anyone who had ever lived. I was afraid of offending my grandfather, or not hearing him, or not understanding what he said, or of having nothing to say. I sat on the edge of the seat and leaned forward as he milked his choke, looking over at him for as long as I could and then looking down momentarily as if maybe listening to the engine as it warmed up, learning it as he knew it.

There was no one awake in my grandparents' house as we backed out of the driveway into the darkness and mist. The house was big and dark and inviting-looking. He had awakened me with a push at my shoulder. Then in the dark, as I headed to the bathroom, he spoke.

"Ever find it hard getting up in the morning?" He laughed, softly and gruffly at the same time. I rubbed my eyes and smiled at him. He was teasing me about waking up and I didn't need to say anything back. I was in my late teens when, in an unbidden replaying of that morning in my mind, I was all at once aware that he was saying something else to me, wanting to joke with me before I knew how.

We ate oatmeal he had ready, with brown sugar and milk. Then toast. We'd put the rods in the car the night before. He said people had no idea how good the fishing was this far into the fall. "Land sakes, Daniel, don't take that boy out in the cold," my grandmother told him, futilely.

We set the oatmeal dishes in the sink. From the stove—in the dark it glowed across its back panel like a spaceship—he poured coffee while I waited. Then he poured another cup and gave it to me. "Well, I..." was as far as I got. He was headed outside. I followed him through the dark and to the Ford, holding the cup far out in front of me so it sloshed onto the ground instead of my shoes. My jacket was a blue Navy-surplus deck jacket, the best jacket I've ever owned. Next to the Ford was the big new Oldsmobile that my grandfather drove when he went with my grandmother or with my family, or when he went to work. He was the editor of the newspaper, and worked in an office next to the river that came in through the edge of town after pausing to be the lake that we were going to fish in. Inside the house they all slept—my mother and father, my brother and sister and my grandmother—none of the rest of them invited out into the cold morning. They were warm and safe in the big soft beds my grandparents had, inside a house that had the biggest television I'd seen and a room full of dusty board games in the basement.

We drove a few blocks and he stopped the car and got out. I sat, leaning toward the door, reaching for it and then pulling back, not knowing what to do, and sure that whatever I did would be the wrong thing.

"Come on and get the flashlight," he called from behind the car.

At the trunk, I aimed it on the rods. He reached for the light and redirected my hand to shine it into the corner of the trunk. There was a bottle there, and a wrinkled paper bag. He grabbed the bottle and the bag and walked away from the car. I had an idea then—to shine the light just ahead of where he was walking. No one had told me this, or shown me. I thought of it then, and was proud, and then wondered what I had done with the coffee.

"You don't remember this, do you?" my grandfather said as we walked away from the car.

"No," I said. *The place? The dark? The bottle?*

"Last time we fished when the bait store wasn't open

you were maybe five or six," he said. "It was daylight, and you did the squeezing."

"Shine it down," he said. He reached into the bag and then I remembered something. A smell. In the bag was a rubber syringe. I remembered more, having it in my hand. He uncapped the bottle and the smell was there—stronger than the cigarette smell. Mustard, it was. You squeezed the syringe, then stuck it down into the bottle and then unsqueezed. It filled up with the mustard water.

"These right here look good," he said. I hadn't been aware that he had the light, but he shined it just away from my feet, at a cluster of five or six holes as big around as a pencil. Around each hole was a collection of six or eight tiny round black balls of black dirt, the size of a BB. And less round. I knew what to do. I squatted, pushed the end of the syringe into one of the holes and squeezed some of the mustard water into the hole.

"Not quite so much in each one," he said. I stopped squeezing and moved to the next hole. I emptied the syringe on the fourth hole. I filled the syringe again and looked back down. A long dark worm was coming out of the first hole I'd squirted. The worm squirmed hard, and came out fast. My grandfather laughed and grunted at the same time. He reached with the same grip he'd used on the choke—strong and soft at the same time—to pull the worm out. He put it into his coffee cup and then kneeled down to scrape at the soil with his hand, to put some in with the worm. I could hear what my grandmother would say if she saw the worm and the dirt in her coffee cup. She'd say his name high and loud, with an edge that sounded like real anger, like when one of her grandchildren came in with muddy shoes. "Let's don't do that," she'd say to us, as if she'd been doing it too.

My coffee had been on the floor of the car, and I sipped it on the ride out to the boat. The closest taste that I knew to the coffee was a pencil when you chewed it just below the eraser. It was still dark when we got to the boat. I wondered what time it was. There were more rituals at the boat than there had been with the worms. But I had been in the boat back in the summer, and so I knew more of them, and could sometimes anticipate what I needed to do. It was a twelve-foot boat that he had built from a kit, with a tiny motor at the back. My grandfather said nothing as we worked, as if saving all the words he could, or getting ready for the silence he demanded when we fished. Only once—when his cigarette fell out of his mouth and into the wet bottom of the boat and hissed quickly at him as he stepped on— did I hear the short, soft, deep-in-the-throat noise that conveyed his deepest dismays. He made the noise at the table when someone chewed with his mouth open.

When the light was full enough that you could see all the way across the lake, we had caught five brim, two perch and one catfish. He caught all of them except two brim. He squinted up at the sky as if it were much brighter than it was, and then started the engine. I assumed we were headed to a new cove to fish, but at the head of the cove he took us into—I had sat in the cold and listened to the drone of the little engine for what seemed like half an hour—he aimed the boat straight in toward the shore. As happened twenty times a day with him, I was frightened and excited at the same time. Maybe he would crash the boat to see if I would help save it. Or take us in to build a fire and cook the fish. He cut the engine and let the boat push its way onto the shore.

"When we go back to fish later, you can run the engine," he said. We got out and he carried the fish—

thrown into a metal bucket where they occasionally made furious splashing noises—with us, up a long hill, along a narrow path that appeared would go on forever. Sticker bushes and low trees grew everywhere as we climbed, breathing hard, until all at once there was a flat spot of bare, red-clay earth.

"Look here," my grandfather said. There were big piles of cinder blocks off to one side of the cleared space. Some of the blocks had been cemented into a low rectangle, the start of a building, I decided. "This is the place . . ." he began to me, but stopped when a truck drove up next to us from along a dirt road I hadn't imagined to have been there. "He's almost on time," my grandfather said.

The man who got out of the truck looked older than my grandfather, about the same height, but much heavier. His stomach stretched the front of his white tee shirt down over his belt.

"Mookie," my grandfather said.

"Danny," the man said. I had never heard anyone call him Danny. He was Mr. Coggins when we went into town, Daniel or Dan to my grandmother, Daddy to my mother and Dandad to my brother and sister and me, though I never called him anything. "And a little Danny too."

"Alex," my grandfather said. "This is Alex and he's out here to work his hind-end off today." *Work at what?*

"Let's get to it," my grandfather said to Mookie.

Mookie looked up at the sky. "Good-lookin' day." He reached into his back pocket and pulled out a small container a slightly shinier color than the bucket and took a short sip from it. He gestured toward my grandfather, who shook his head gently.

"Let's go," Mookie said.

While the sun came up out of the trees and then got

clouded over, the three of us worked at the cinder blocks. I carried them to the foundation one at a time and my grandfather and Mookie used trowels to coat one edge with cement my grandfather mixed in an old wheelbarrow that didn't have wheels or one of the handles. At the times he mixed cement, Mookie did the troweling by himself. Mookie was the first to have to pee and all he did was turn and barely miss the pile of blocks where I was working. "Not quite cold enough for much steam," he said as his long stream made a strong noise off the soil, "but I'll take either one of you on for distance."

Later he reached into his mouth and pulled out one of his teeth and let a long white string come out of his mouth behind it as he held out the tooth. He spit more often than anyone I'd ever seen, and he drank from the little silver container every little while. He made long loud noises in his throat that I thought might irritate my grandfather, but he didn't say anything to Mookie about it.

My grandfather didn't talk to either one of us much except to keep us working. Once during the morning, when Mookie was back at his truck, my grandfather walked over to me and talked about Mookie. "Mookie lost his brother in a train wreck when they were nineteen," he said suddenly. "His twin brother, it was. The brother was a good ballplayer and was in his second year in professional baseball. Mookie was trying to catch up to a freight train that his brother had already hopped, on their way to a ball game, and he reached out of the car and down to pull Mookie up. But the train was picking up speed too fast, and Mookie's brother got pulled out of the train. Mookie let go as his brother was falling out and the momentum of being pulled, I guess it was, threw Mookie's brother under the edge of the car and onto the tracks."

My grandfather told it fast, as if to get it out of the way. I looked at him with no idea what to say. He looked up toward the truck to see where Mookie was. "He's worked with me off and on ever since," my grandfather said. He looked again. "You know the fireplace out back from the house?" Midway in my grandfather's back yard was a rock fireplace that looked like a little castle. It backed up against the hill. He burned brush in it. I told him I did know it. "Mookie built that maybe twenty-five years ago." I remembered the only time I knew of when my grandfather and my father seemed to be angry with each other. We were in the back yard, and there was corn, wrapped in aluminum foil, roasting in that fireplace. "This fireplace is really a bit out of kilter, Dan, isn't it?" my father said. He tilted his head to one side, as if judging it. My grandfather made the beginning of a throat noise and walked right past my father toward the house, saying nothing. My mother and grandmother followed him in, in a hurry.

As we worked into the morning, the clouds became thicker and thicker, and as the wind got stronger it turned cold. My grandfather asked Mookie if he had the lunch, and Mookie said it wasn't his turn to bring the lunch.

"Mook, Mook, Mook," my grandfather said. "I told you I was coming in the boat today, remember?"

Mookie looked down toward the lake. "Fuck," he said. It was the first time I'd heard an adult say that. Strong and sharp, it was, into the cold air. Mookie looked back at his truck. "Let me check," he said, but you could tell he knew better.

My grandfather looked at me. "You want to cook the fish?" he said. "If we do, that means we have to be sure to catch more later to have some to take back. We can't go back to town empty-handed."

"Sure," I said. He sent me to look for small twigs to

start a fire. Mookie came back from the truck with a big jar. It was half full of what I assumed to be water. He smiled broadly as he brought it. As I put down a load of twigs, he asked me if I wanted some. He held the big jar and tipped it toward my lips. I jumped away when I tasted it, spilling some. He and my grandfather laughed.

"Moonshine," Mookie said with a big smile. "Mookie's own magic 'shine."

"It'll eat your insides out, Alex," my grandfather said.

My grandfather's lighter kept blowing out because of the wind. Finally he got the leaves to catch, and then the twigs. Then he took out his knife to clean the fish. A gust came and blew the fire out of its spot. He told me to put a few of the blocks next to the fire spot and try again. He threw his lighter to me and then told me to put the blocks on the other side—the side the wind was coming from. It was cold. I picked up the lighter I had almost caught, and then there was a clap of thunder that made me jump more than the moonshine had. I had almost caught the lighter, and while I had tried to figure out how I'd missed it, too many things had happened in a row for me to keep up with very well. I licked my finger and put it up to be sure about the wind. Both my grandfather and Mookie laughed.

It took maybe half an hour to get the fire to where it had enough heat and coals to cook anything. My grandfather had cut twigs from trees—twigs with forks at the end. He laid a piece of fish over the fork of one and handed it to me. I was unsure.

"Roast it," Mookie said immediately. "Like a hotdog only don't turn it and let it fall off."

I held the stick out toward the fire and worried about it catching on fire. Soon Mookie and my grandfather were doing the same thing. I watched when they grabbed the fish and turned it over without burning themselves.

"Indians," my grandfather said as he lifted a big

chunk of perch off his stick to eat it. "We could be Indians out here in the wild, you know it, boys?"

"They was all through here," Mookie said. "Toteros and Cherokees and all." He swept his hand widely around in front of him.

"How do you know that, Mook?" my grandfather said.

Mookie pointed at his head. "There's still a little left up here," he said, and smiled. He took a bite of his own fish.

We ate all the fish. My grandfather and I didn't drink anything, and Mookie took two or three gulps from the big jar. There was a short time as we all still sat on cinder blocks and the fire was still going and nobody was saying anything. In the middle of this, snow began to come out of the wind. There were a few flakes for a moment, and before any of us could say anything about it, the snow was heavy all around us. Mookie let out a squeal and took a long sip out of his jar. My grandfather stood up and walked over to the foundation. Three of the walls were now about as tall as I was, and part of one wall as tall as the men. The flakes hit one wall from the side and left little dark spots on the cinder blocks. The snow was thick enough just then that you could look down toward the lake and not see it. I wondered if it would snow a foot and we would have a hard time driving back once we took the boat back to the car. I thought about my mother for the first time that day—that she would stand at the window back at my grandparents' house and call out to everyone to look at the snow coming down. But as I thought that, the snow stopped.

My grandfather went over to Mookie and put his arm around his shoulder.

"You think we've done enough for today, Mook?" he said.

"We could be under a foot of snow here directly," Mookie said, and laughed.

My grandfather smiled, and patted Mookie's back as he slid his arm off it. "I expect you're right, Mook," he said.

There were little patches of sunlight in the wind now, and still a flurry here and there. Mookie stood off from the wall, in his tee shirt, and holding the big bottle in one hand, between his thumb and his fingers. There was just a little left now, across the bottom as the jar tilted in his hand. He looked like a little boy to me. My grandfather reached into his back pocket and pulled out his wallet. He counted bills and handed them to Mookie. Mookie took them, put them in his pants pocket and then looked at my grandfather like he might cry.

"Nobody like you in the damn world, Danny," he said.

"You keep that thing out of the ditch," my grandfather said to Mookie, gesturing toward the truck. "Remember, I'm in the boat, so there's no one behind you to pull you out."

Mookie gave my grandfather a military salute. "Y'all boys go back and fish the lake," he laughed, "in snow and thunder at the same time." He walked up to his truck and drove away.

Back at the boat, I wanted to ask my grandfather what time it was. I thought about it a long time, and counted to ten several times to get up the nerve.

"Just after three," he said. "You're not running down are you?"

"No," I said, telling the truth.

"Because if you are," he said, "if you are, well, too bad. We've got to replace the fish we ate up." He laughed easily, looking straight at me.

It was cold on the lake. The water was ripply, and my grandfather had apparently forgotten that I was to run the boat. Twice as he aimed us through the cold, there were gusts that changed the boat's direction slightly. I looked back at my grandfather each time, and he kept looking on ahead, as if nothing had happened. We went back to the cove where we'd caught most of the fish and drifted back under the trees that reached out from the steep bank. There were still brown leaves on some of them.

The cove was so sheltered that the wind was almost gone, but the trees and clouds brought an early edge of darkness that made it feel later than I guessed it was. My grandfather caught a big catfish almost as soon as we dropped the anchor. As they nearly always did, the catfish swallowed the hook, and I watched my grandfather get out his knife and work at the fish. His hands were strong and soft at the same time, pulling at the line, cutting deep into the fish's throat, holding the fish strong around its midsection. Just before he finished, I caught a big perch. Then each of us caught a brim. My grandfather laughed then.

"Two fishin' fools out here in the cold," he said. Up at his end of the boat, he reached into his big tackle box and pulled out two cans of Falstaff beer. He threw one to me, and I caught it. He used his knife to punch two holes in the top of his and then threw me the knife. I caught the knife too, and after I tried to punch into the can, he stood up and I handed him my can to open. He felt big, standing there next to me. The boat was still and the bobbers were still as he handed me back the can with two holes in it.

The beer was worse than the coffee, but not as bad as the moonshine. There was a sensation in my mouth that seemed like it might be Dr. Pepper, but then the taste turned bad. I looked down at my grandfather, glancing at his can and then at mine. On some Saturdays in the summer, we watched the baseball game on television, and between innings, Dizzy Dean and Peewee Reese said that Falstaff was good beer. It was worse than medicine, and I drank it more slowly than I had the coffee.

"They don't know about the building back at home," my grandfather said then, after a sip of his beer. "They know we went fishing today, and when we take home whatever we catch now, I guess we had a pretty bad day." He laughed.

I looked down at him through the twilight at his end of the boat. I had just caught a good fish. I had a can of beer in my hand. I wasn't shivering anymore. "Why don't they know?" I said, feeling strong.

"About the building?" he said. "They will, but there's no hurry. Sometimes your grandmother worries too much about things. About our money and your family and about Mookie when she hears about him. Some things are better to get done without telling her all about it. Some things are better going slowly. Lots of things with women." He paused then, and winked a real wink. "Even your own momma, with a new baby coming, is a little more worried about things she doesn't need to be." *We were having a new baby?*

"Or fishing. You know you have to be patient and coax things along just at the right speed. You get a bite and you jerk too hard you won't get the fish, right?"

I nodded at him.

"What is the building?" I said. I sipped the beer right then and it tasted slightly less bad.

"It's a cabin," he said. "When you come to visit next summer when school's out, it should be finished, and we can come up to the lake—all of us—and sleep in it. Fish and swim and play down by the water with a brand new baby." He laughed

I thought of the long walk up to the cinder blocks from the lake, about cutting a better trail through there. I knew my grandfather would do that. Maybe he and Mookie would do it, or maybe I would help. "So nobody knows?" I said to my grandfather.

He pulled the rope to start the motor just as I said that. He looked at me as the motor struggled to start. I realized he'd pulled in his fishing line, and I reeled mine in quickly.

"What?" he shouted over the motor.

"Nobody else knows?" I shouted back. The engine sputtered then, and he turned to it, grabbing at the throttle quickly and revving it even higher to keep it from stalling.

"About the cabin?" he said. His hand was wrapped around the throttle the same way he'd held the choke on the Ford in the morning. He was easing the speed of the motor gently down as its running smoothed out. He looked at me as he did this, and I could tell he was listening to the engine and I was not to talk again just yet. Once the engine was calm under his cupped hand, he spoke again.

"You and me and Mookie," he said. "We're the only ones who know and Mookie never tells anyone anything." He took the last sip of his beer, put the can in his tackle box and lit a new cigarette. He glanced around at the boat, as if to make sure we were ready to go, and then looked at me hard. "You and me and Mookie," he said again, over the quieter engine noise.

"You and me and Mookie," I called back to him. I tried to look at him the same way he looked at me—straight and hard—as if to tell him I understood him. I took another sip of the beer and looked around the boat, to help him check. He stood up then, and motioned for me to come back to where the engine was. As we moved past each other to change ends, the boat listed slightly to his side, and we reached instinctively for each other. He grabbed me by the shoulders. As I held the thick muscle of his biceps, I smelled smoke and fish and cold and cement from him. As we let go and moved to opposite ends of the little boat, I could feel something high in my chest, something I was too young and too cold to recognize as love.

Cold

This is New Year's Eve day, on the ice just off a little spit of land into the upper Chesapeake Bay, northeast of Baltimore. It is eight in the morning, and my brother and I are sitting on the long, warped-wood dock out over the cove that reaches into our neighborhood with a round, pleasing shape. We are lacing up black figure skates, with metal eyelets and then hooks that reach halfway to our knees. Brian is eleven and I am sixteen. We have not said anything to each other since well before we left the house to walk down here to the cove, but now, amid lacing, we have things to say. It is ritual talking, though we don't know it—as if sitting on the pier to lace skates calls for talking. You could stand at the head of the pier and watch all day, and you'd see that everybody—pulling up his pantleg to get to work—talks to whoever is sitting nearby doing the same. Brian says he saw that it was six on the thermometer outside the kitchen window. I tell him that the high for the whole day is only going to be eighteen and that the ice is at least two feet thick. He says it already looks like low tide even though it should be high tide about now. I tell him there is no sign of an end to the cold. Back and forth we go, just as our laces do across the front of our legs, each seeking the bigger number, the better winter fact.

Next to each of us is a treasure—what we use as our hockey sticks. Mine is a perfect limb I found and then sawed and planed and sanded to look and act more like a real stick than anyone else's. Brian's is a worn broom that our mother took her pinking shears to, forming a head that is better for cradling than for a slap shot. Our father was aghast at the waste of a broom and Brian was pleased with the shape. The ice has been thick enough to skate on for six days in a row, and every day Brian and I have been the first ones to the cove. Two days we brought little Cannon with us to skate in the morning, but now he has a cold and has to stay home. Cannon is three and already a good skater. Cannon is the only thing Brian and I agree on, except hockey sometimes.

Some years we go the whole winter and get no more than two or three days to skate, and the ice is thin and rough and uncertain. This winter the temperature has not been above freezing for the whole week we have been out of school, and the sun seems to stay lower than ever as it arcs its way across the sky, as if God is on our side. As I finish tying I stand immediately, feeling my power as a skater and verifying that I am just as tall as I was yesterday with skate blades under me. The blades make a tonky noise across the remaining planks of pier to where you lower yourself down a support pole onto the ice.

Out on the ice, dragging our sticks like players on the way to the penalty box, Brian and I make big loops and skate backwards and cut into the ice with the toe-teeth of our skates—putting on all the moves we know to show off for each other without saying anything.

Brian got new skates for Christmas and bragged they were only one size smaller than mine. Now he is not bragging, but carrying out every move I do on the clear piece of ice we have picked.

"Guys should be here," he says while we are going backwards, next to each other. "It's late."

"No lie," I tell him.

The sun is still low and new enough that the cove has a yellow-gray tint. Up at our end—near the houses—the ice is scarred to white where we have had good games. Each day we move a little farther out, edging like pioneers with endless land—to start a new game on new, clean, uncut ice.

People arrive slowly, casually walking onto the pier carrying their skates as if they're only considering actually putting them on. From the ice I watch them with a deep impatience that manifests itself in slapping at Brian with my stick and yelling out to people to hurry up. By the time we are ready to really play there are enough skaters for seven on one side and six on the other. Almost everyone is either about Brian's age or about my age, as if the demographics of cove hockey are narrowed to people with either the confidence of being the kings of the elementary school or the uncertainty of being just into high school. The good balance of both age groups makes it easy to create relatively even teams.

"Me, Brian, Stan, Henny, Carroll and Stoof against the rest of you," I try.

"Every day you try that crap," my friend Richard says. "And every day we have to remind you that you and Brian—since you're out here approximately twenty-four hours a damn day, and also have the best sticks and the newest skates—are not going to be on the same team."

I look at my skates, exuding incredulousness. "These are beat to heck," I say, "and Brian's little broom does better with dust than a puck." Most of the others have a broom or a mop or a hand-made stick that will as likely as not come loose at the joint where it was nailed and then taped. There is one player—a sixteen year-old who is the worst on the ice and also the only one who has actual hockey skates on—who got a hockey stick for Christmas, as if he knew the ice was coming but not that he would need to know how to skate too.

Next we take time to find the sticks and limbs we put behind the goals so we don't have to spend half the game time skating halfway out into the Chesapeake to retrieve the puck, which is also courtesy of the boy with the real skates and stick. The game is at the mouth of the cove, with one goal at the end of the longest, tallest pier anywhere around the whole peninsula. In the summer there are huge sailboats and motorboats tied to it. Now there are big planks of ice that have broken into chunks as big as ironing boards and thick as lumber. They lean against the poles of the dock where the falling tide has left them—part of the huge and cold of the winter.

The game settles quickly into people pushing and leaning, and the puck shooting out to one side or the other—far out into the big finger of the bay beyond us or back into the cove. We retrieve it and drop it between us and go at it again. We go perhaps longer than we have all week without a score, and you can feel people beginning to lose intensity. Just after a near score for my side, as the puck is put back in play, it pops up in the air near Brian, who cradles it while it's still airborne—using his broom head with a move none of us has ever seen—and carries it in the air for three or four quick strides—running on the toe teeth of his skates—before he lets the puck fall to the ice and begins long, fast skating strides. He's well out ahead of our defense and on his way for an open shot. Our goalie is a guy Brian's age—smaller and far less coordinated than Brian—and there is almost no doubt Brian will score. I am after him from the time that he does his air move, and just as he is drawing his broom back to either fake the goalie to one side or actually take his shot, I draw within reaching distance of him. I do not stop to think about this, but the only chance I have to stop him is to reach with my stick. I swing it from above and his right, getting just the tip of it in front of his right skate. The wood of my stick hits the front of his skate blade and stops the skate's movement. I feel the pull at my arm, and go down onto the ice rather than let the stick be pulled out of my hand. Brian's fall is far more spectacular, as the little wooden chock suddenly stuck in front of his skate has the effect of the left side of his body trying to continue forward while the right side is brought to an immediate halt. He spins for what seems to be three full revolutions before he falls, head first and into the goalie—the puck continuing weakly off to the side from his fake stroke and his broomstick sliding off to the other side. Brian and the goalie form a pile that continues to slide through the goal, into the sticks and brush and on across the ice for thirty feet.

Long before they have stopped sliding, Brian is screaming at me about the dirtiest play he's ever seen, about how I could have killed somebody, and if a hockey game means that much to me then I should move to Canada. It is part embarrassment and part just the look of Brian and Tommy sliding across the ice in one heap while Brian is screaming that makes me laugh. I am skating slowly toward Brian, who is trying furiously to stop his slide so he can come back after me. I reach him about the time they come to a stop and reach down to extend him a hand up, and ask him if he's okay. He hits at my hand with his fist, and then reaches behind him for one of the branches he and Tommy have been pushing. He is swinging at me—with the intensity that only a little brother angry at his big brother can have—as hard as he can with a branch that still has leaves on it. The leaves have the effect of slowing how fast he can swing it. I laugh again.

Brian and I spend perhaps nearly a minute in that balance; he is furious and helpless and I am half-amused/half pitying, and neither of us can get a full grip on his emotions. Suddenly, still seated on the ice as I move nearby but out of branch-swinging range, he begins unlacing one of his skates.

"What are you doing, Brian?" I ask him, skating easily. "What is he doing?" I turn to say to others, who are in a cluster behind us.

Brian's face is a twisted blend of red and white skin. His fury seems to boil from within and be not quite able to escape. His mouth makes little puffy shapes and little puffy sounds, but no more words are coming out. He pulls at the loosened skate to try to take it off, causing him to slip momentarily onto his back and me to try to stifle more laughter. Finally the skate comes off. He stands then, on one skate and one socked foot. I have no idea even as he draws his arm back, what he is about to do. He plants with the teeth of his right skate and throws the left skate at me as hard as he can. I am only a few feet away, my arms at my sides and my face still broken with a smile. My hand is up by the time the skate reaches me. The blade hits the fleshy part of my right palm, sliding and cutting just beneath the glove as it does. The leather top of the skate—with laces and eyelets—smacks into my face at what seems to be the same moment that the pain registers in my hand and that I feel my feet going out from under me. As soon as I am on the ice, Brian is on top of me, pummeling away at my head with both fists.

Neither Brian nor I has a watch, but you can look at the light beginning to drain out of the sky, at the deep shadows in the coves far across the ice, and know that it's getting close to four o'clock. With the time we've had waiting for people to come back, we have scouted all the way across the big stretch of ice over to the edge of the land that holds neighborhoods that take half an hour to drive to. We found a piece of two-by-four that must be twelve feet long, and two other big pieces of lumber that make perfect puck-stops behind the goal. We found better markers—two old buoy flags and another part of flag and a piece of sail that was just barely hanging on a boat that had been left in the water for the winter—for the goals. With the new behind-goal wood we found, we took the branches and sticks we've used for that purpose all week and strung them around the whole perimeter of the field, to create an enclosed hockey rink. It is long and wide and completely surrounded.

"Why say you're coming back if you're not?" Brian says. His voice surprises me through the cold, as neither of us has said anything since people went home, soon after the fight.

I try to talk myself out of looking back down into the cove every few seconds, making deals with myself that if I wait five minutes, then when I look again, there will be people on the dock lacing up skates. But I am unable to keep my head from turning to look every few seconds. "Going home to get something to eat is one thing, but I mean . . ." I tell Brian, and then tail off.

"Right," he says. "If you're too much of a wimp to

make it all day or bring along a sandwich, then fine, go home. But don't say you're coming back if you're not."

Back near the beginning of the week, after one day of getting in trouble for keeping Cannon out too long and another for not going home for lunch, our mother told us we had three choices: come home to eat; take food with us; or she would come down to the cove, put on her skates and come out to get us if we didn't come when she called. We told her there was no place to put food. It would get crushed in our coats. She told us to hide it under the pier where it connects to the land. We protested we would look like girls or something, hiding food. She asked us weren't we always the first ones there? And didn't everyone else go home at least for a little while? Our cheese sandwiches the last two days have been crunchy with the freezing temperatures, but we have not had to leave the ice except to tonk back up along the pier to get the sandwiches and our canteens, which disappoint us because the water is not quite frozen solid.

When Brian was hitting me as we were both on the ice after he threw his skate, he stopped suddenly, with one arm up in the air, ready to strike again. "Alex, you're all cut," he said in a wail. "There's blood pouring out of your hand." He grabbed at my hand to show me, and as I sat up, other skaters moved in to take a look, talking about losing too much blood, and raising it up in the air, and going home to see about stitches. I wiped at the cut with one of the gloves. I could see that the cut was just a sort of opening-up of the flesh, like a biology dissection at school—maybe three inches long and less than an eighth of an inch deep. I told people it wasn't bad, and when they continued to talk about stopping the bleeding, I took my jacket and shirt off, and then my tee shirt. I put the shirt and jacket back on and then tore a long strip from the soft white tee shirt and wrapped it around my hand. I knew that if I went home, everyone else would too, and it would be an hour, or two hours, before we could get back to playing. Once my hand was wrapped and I pulled the glove on as far as it would go—to where my fingers met my hand—I told everyone we could get going again. But the time we'd lost and the busting up of one of the goals seemed to have taken the momentum out of the game. And as always, once one person started home, others took it as permission, and soon everyone except Brian and me was moving toward the pier, talking about it already being past lunch time anyway. Tommy, the only one with a watch, said it was twenty till two. Brian talked to the guys his age and I did to those mine, seeking a commitment to being back no later than two-thirty.

"That's plenty of time to eat and take a crap and change your socks and bring Alex a couple new tee shirts for his gusher," Brian said. People laughed and said they'd be back.

Now—what seems like many hours later—Brian and I skate easily near the hockey rink we have created. For awhile we passed the puck back and forth inside, and took a few easy shots on open goals. Then we hopped over the barrier we created and skated out toward the bay a distance, as if creating the amount of time it would take to have people come back. Now we are in close to the pier.

"Look at the cove," Brain says as we move toward it. "The tide's so low it looks like the ice is right on top of the mud—it's all sunk down in the middle."

I tell Brian he's right—that this is the lowest tide we've seen yet. "I think it's a combination of the cold and the moon," I tell him.

"Yeah," he says. "Zero tonight, or below."

We drift toward the middle of our cove, where we have skated every time there was ice for as long as we can remember—since just after we could walk. The light seems to change as we get back to our home ice—back to the gray-yellow we saw in the morning, but with orange mixed in. The sky is starting to look slatey and the ice too, so that your breath looks whiter than ever when you puff it out to see it against those steely-gray backdrops.

"We had one more game," Brian says and then cuts to a quick stop, looks down, and tells me to look too. "It's shad," he says. "Those real big orange ones you see out in the lagoon. Tons."

I skate next to him—stopping at the middle of the cove where he has stopped—and look down at the ice. Big orange shapes are moving—far more slowly than fish move—under the ice.

"There's no water left toward the edge of the cove—just what's right under us here in the middle," Brian says. "They're trapped."

"You're right." I sit down on the ice and start chopping at it with the long back end of my skate blade. Brian sits down and does the same. The ice is hard, and pieces break away and fly up quickly. It is not long before the blade goes down into the hole it has chopped and doesn't cut any deeper. You can feel the back of your heel hitting the ice.

"You have to make it bigger around," Brian says.

"Or else we need something better to chop with." I get up and skate in toward the pier, looking for a metal stake or rod or something else that I know I would have remembered while sitting on the ice if it had been there to see. I get up on the pier and walk back to the shore, to look around the pier's edges. "Somebody could've left an anchor from the summer," I call out to Brian. He stops chopping to ask me what I said. I call out that there ought to be something up along the shore to chop with.

"I'm close," he calls back. "It really is shad under there, and they can hardly move. I'm almost hitting them on the head and they just sort of sit there."

I get back on the ice and skate out to Brian. He has chopped a hole nearly as big around as a garbage can lid at the top, and narrowing down to the size of a bucket where he is starting to get little splashes of water when his skate blade hits.

"Watch this," he says when I am back beside him. He chops with his skate blade and then holds it up in the air.

"What?" I ask him impatiently. I am looking at the fish. If his hole were just a little deeper, you could reach down and touch them.

"The blade," he says. "Look at it—the water freezes on it before it can run off. It is *cold* out here, Alex."

I tell him he's right. The end of his skate blade has a thin, whitish cake of ice on it. I tell him to take a deep breath through his nose to see if it freezes.

"God, it does," he says. He does his water-to-ice chop again and it works again. He tells me to go get a stick for the fish, and I skate back to the pier where I saw a piece of broken plank while Brian goes back to chopping the last little way through.

He is on his knees when I get back, looking down into his hole. He reaches for the stick and I hand it to him, without thought. At the bottom of the hole, big orange fish—almost two feet long—move around in slow small movements. Brian puts the end of the stick on the back of one and pushes it. It doesn't swim away the way fish do. It just moves with the stick. "They must be frozen," Brian says. "If the tide goes any lower and there won't be enough water left—they'll be frozen right into the mud."

"I think they might die anyway," I tell Brian. "Who ever heard of fish moving that slow."

"I don't think they'll die," he says. "I mean they've been under there all this time, all this cold weather. For years, or they wouldn't be this big."

"Unless chopping the hole makes that water under there freeze too," I say.

Brian looks up, worried. "No," he says, sort of hopefully. "It'll just freeze over the top where I chopped and be just like it was."

I look at him and shrug.

"Let's fill it back in then," he says, and turns the stick on its side to push the little accumulation of ice choppings back toward the hole. Then he stops and looks up. "You want to touch one first?" he says, holding out the stick.

I start to take the stick, thinking about pushing a big slow fish down deeper into the water—down closer to the mud. I know exactly what it will feel like—the slow, squishy give of a cold cold fish. "No, go ahead," I tell him. "Fill it in."

Brian works from his knees, using the stick as a little snow plow to put the ice back into the hole. He works even faster than he did with the chopping, and in hardly any time, the ice looks almost the way it did before he started at it with his blade. It is whitish and only slightly smooth—the same way it had gotten from all our games on it.

Brian stands up when he is finished, next to me there in the middle of our cove as the day turns a deeper and deeper purple around us. "You think we should get some of that brush and stuff from the rink and cover where the hole was?" Brian says.

"What for?"

"You know, more warmth and all."

"You think that brush is sending any heat down

through all that ice you got another thing coming," I tell Brian softly. "Plus, that's a hockey rink you and I built out there, man. No way we're going to tear it down before we get to play on it."

Brian looks out that way and smiles. "If they could see that rink, they'd be back in no time," he says.

"I think that edge would stop almost anything except you and Tommy hitting it at ninety miles an hour," I say to Brian. I glance over at the dock again, feeling suddenly certain there will be three or four guys on the pier, lacing up their skates. It is getting so dusky that I have to squint to make sure there really is no one there.

"How's your hand?" Brian says. He has skated up right next to me.

"Good," I say, and twist it toward me to look at the red spot on the cloth that covers that hand. Then I turn it toward him for his look.

"You catch a baseball a little better than you catch an ice skate," Brian says. He pushes me then, almost knocking me over. As I catch myself to keep from falling backwards, I am laughing, and wondering how Brian could say that to me and shove me at the same time and not have me get angry. He makes a big-eyed face at me as I steady myself, and then grins as he skates away backwards, slowly.

This is my little brother, is what I think then. I feel this so palpably that I am aware of it rising from my chest into my face. We are out here together in the freezing cold while it is getting dark on the last day of the year and nobody else in the world is even thinking about ice or cold fish or skating. Everybody we know has either not come down at all for the whole day, or has gone home and started to put on fancy clothes or gone to visit people or to break out the egg nog, leaving Brian and me alone on the ice for the whole afternoon to discover every piece of the wondrous cold that has suddenly made me see him in some way new. The darkness is drawing quickly down upon us, enshrouding us on this one cold spot together—linking us best, as will happen for as long as we live, in the cold.

Soup for Cannon

In November, on a Friday long ago, in a war-worker neighborhood built twenty years earlier on low, swampy land northeast of Baltimore, my baby brother and I are in the kitchen. He is five, I am eighteen, and we are the only two left in the house, one of scores just like it, all within less than a mile of the airplane factory buildings. Lisa and Brian, the sister and brother who fall between our ages, are at school. My mother is at work in the city, at another school. My father, who works at yet another school, lives in a different house, six blocks away. We moved out of the old house and into the one he bought for my mother a year or so back.

"You want the cereal again, Can?" I say to my brother. He woke up much later than he usually does, but I know he'll still want breakfast. The sun makes a plank across the edge of the shiny-topped kitchen table. The silver legs that support the table slant slightly outward on their way to the floor, and are cold even in the summer when it's a hundred degrees. Sitting at the table and waiting for Cannon to answer me, I grab one of the legs with both hands, curling my fingers around it the way I would a baseball bat. I like the feel of the cold metal.

"The cereal," he says. We never had boxes of cereal until the last two weeks. But the three of us older than Cannon—Lisa is sixteen and Brian thirteen—told him that if he asked Mom enough times then we would get cereal like we have when we visit our grandmother in Virginia. On those visits, every night she eats a big bowl of corn flakes with vanilla ice cream on top of the cereal and cut up banana on top of the ice cream. We told Cannon to tell Mom we wouldn't ask for the ice cream, or even the bananas, and that the cereal would help us all get more milk. She brought the cereal home from the grocery store the very next time she went. Lisa said part of the reason she got it was because our father wasn't around to see it. He wanted you to eat oatmeal every day.

Cannon sits in his chair atop a big dictionary and a telephone book. I pour cereal into his bowl, watching the little O-shaped pieces roll in, and think about if they have anything to do with the Baltimore Orioles, the best baseball team in the world. Then I pour milk over the Os and slide the bowl directly under Cannon's face, reach back into the drawer, grab a spoon and slide it toward him so it stops right next to the bowl. "There y'go, chief," I tell Cannon, proud of my athletic motions with dishes and of my ability to take care of him and be in charge of a whole house. I look out the window for the mailman and to see if any of the neighbors' cars are still parked on the street or if Mrs. Randall from next door is out in her front yard.

Cannon looks up at me with a smile, the same way he does twenty times a day. I am too young to understand the huge and vulnerable love of a brother almost thirteen years younger, but I know it on some level and drink it in every day.

What will happen next in the late morning—maybe even before Cannon is finished eating—is that Elaine will come to the house. Elaine is sixteen and my girlfriend. She lives in a boarding house closer to town, waiting for the first half of the school year to end before she starts again. She went to the Catholic school for girls in the city until she quit and ran away from home after her father called the police because I had come back to visit her at 1:30 in the morning after he told me the day before never to come back to his house again. After Christmas, Elaine will go to school in the county high school where I went and where Lisa goes now. They'll both be juniors.

Cannon slides off his dictionary and telephone book and lands on the floor. He cries. I go pick him up. "Upsy daisy," I say to him, in imitation of my mother, and put him back on his perch. I reach under him and square up his heighteners. "Can, Can, Can," I say and then make a little tsking noise with my tongue and lips. We smile again and then Cannon looks up at the ceiling and shivers one little cry-shiver before he talks.

"Is this the same cereal?" he says.

"Same as what?"

"Same as yesterday."

I grab the box and smack it onto my face to pretend to inspect it, to make Cannon laugh. "Looks the same to me," I say in a voice like Red Skelton's. "Just exactly the same."

Cannon laughs and puts his spoon in his cereal. I wonder then if he will be like Brian, who says he gets tired of eating the same things over and over again. "You like it, don't you, Can?" I say. "You sure liked it yesterday, a couple bowls' worth. Maybe you slept too long to be eating breakfast, little man."

"It tastes kind of funny," he says.

I think, as the only one in the house besides Cannon, things that would never occur to me if my mother were at home. I am in charge of Cannon, after all, on the two days a week I don't have classes at the community college. I went away to college at the beginning of fall, but I came home because of Elaine, in time to take four classes. "Let me check the milk," I say to Cannon. I get the milk out of the refrigerator and sniff it. It's in a glass quart bottle, with a loose-fitting paper cap on it. I put the paper cap back on and tell Cannon it smells okay. Then I walk over and push my nose and face into the side of Cannon's belly, enough to tickle him. "You don't smell that good though," I tell him.

"Maybe I have a temperature?" Cannon says when he is finished laughing.

"We all have a temperature, Can," I say, in echo of my father, "and I doubt you have a fever." Cannon lets his head fall off slightly to the side as if he has understood and wants to wave away the technicality to get to the issue. I put my hand on his little forehead, which feels like any little forehead to me. I wonder how my mother can tell a person's temperature by putting her hand there. "You're fine," I tell him.

After I have given Cannon his head back, he takes two bites of cereal and smiles again. Maybe a little bravely, it occurs to me. I wonder if maybe he really is sick and will take too much of the time that Elaine and I have together while we babysit him. She has to get back on the bus by two o'clock to get to her job at a submarine sandwich shop where the owner, a man from Greece, says he will fire her the first time she is late. Cannon lets his head fall to one side again and I tell him he's going to crash off the chair again if he isn't careful, and then the front door opens and Elaine comes in. She has on a blue jacket and a straight green skirt that is above her knees. It is the best skirt she has. I get up from the table to go hug her, but before I get there, she is talking.

"Cannie's all flushed," she says. She walks past me to Cannon. She puts her hand on his forehead and then pulls his whole head to her chest up near her shoulder, where she sometimes puts my head. "He's burning up," she says to me in an urgent semi-whisper while she's walking to the cabinet near the refrigerator where my mother keeps the medicine. She reaches up into the shelf, pulling the skirt up the back of her legs, and talks back over her shoulder to Cannon at the same time. "How long have you been feeling bad, honey?" she says. I sit back down in my chair and grip the table leg again with both hands. There is no warm spot left from when I held it before.

"I fell off the chair," Cannon says.

"You what?" Elaine looks at me with an expression of dismay, shaking her head and pursing her lips. A few weeks back, when Cannon cut his leg on the fence at the end of the back yard, Elaine acted this same way, though not as strongly. It reminds me of a little girl with dolls, or of a real mother—far older than Elaine—with a real child.

"The books just slipped to the side," I say. "Nothing to do with any fever or me."

Elaine gets a glass of water for Cannon to drink after he takes his medicine. "He really is burning up," she says to me, as if I might have missed it when she said it the first time.

"Where's the thermometer?" Elaine says next. I give Cannon a cross-eyed look that Elaine can't see as I get up to go to the medicine cabinet in the bathroom to get the thermometer.

I can hear Elaine and Cannon talking, murmuring like

nurse and patient out in the kitchen while I am looking for the thermometer. "It's not in here," I call out.

"It *has* to be," Elaine says, her voice moving toward me. She has Cannon in her arms as she comes around the corner, holding him upright so that his head is next to hers and his legs dangle down hers. He is too big to be carried around, but she doesn't seem to mind his weight. I think then, for a reason I don't know, that his name is actually Edwin Hardin, Jr. None of us has ever called him that. When he was a tiny tiny baby, my mother said when he shook his fists he looked like he was trying to fire off a big cannon. She started calling him Cannon right after that, and everyone else has ever since. No one has ever called him Edwin.

When we can't find the thermometer, Elaine says that Cannon is so hot that we need to put him in the bathtub in cool water to make sure his temperature doesn't get dangerously high.

"Ooh, dangerously high," I mimic Elaine.

"I'm serious," she says. "I had a friend at school whose little sister had a fever of a hundred and five and had brain damage."

Cannon's head is now resting on Elaine's shoulder. His face looks red. She sets him down on the toilet seat cover and turns on the water in the tub.

"We're going to make the water kind of cool, Can," she says to him, as if I am not there, "to cool you down a little. It won't be hot and it won't really be cold, but it will feel closer to cold."

Cannon nods slowly and starts to pull his shirt over his head. Elaine reaches to help him. I stand at the bathroom door, leaning against the wall and watching. "I was thinking we were going to get to spend a little time upstairs," I say to Elaine.

"Well I was too, Alex, but we need to take care of him." She doesn't turn to me while she talks, and she puts a little extra emphasis on the word *care*, as if to let me know I am being selfish. "Why don't you go get a story we can read to Cannie while he's in the tub?" she says next.

I go into Cannon's room and look at all the tall, skinny-spined books in a row on his bottom shelf. It has been a long time since anyone read him a story, I think, pulling out books. I am looking for one that has my name printed on a page near the front, in big capital letters too far apart—letters drawn instead of written, by a person too young to write. On the shelf just above the books there is a lot of open space, with just a few tiny metal cars here and there. You can tell that Cannon has placed them just where he wants them. One is parked inside a toothpick box, and another is parked next to a row of four green Monopoly hotels. I straighten a rubber wheel back onto its rim on one of the cars and hope that Cannon is not too sick. I am suddenly glad that Elaine is taking care of him, and feel a swell of love for both of them.

When I get back to the bathroom, Cannon is already in the water, and Elaine is kneeling by the tub, dipping a washcloth in the water and then taking it up on his neck and letting the water run down his back. I sit down on the toilet seat and open the book. The book is "Mr. Bear Squash-You-All-Flat." It is a funny book because it calls the bear *very stupid* when we were not allowed to call anyone stupid, and because the bear keeps squashing things flat until all the little animals move into a tire and Mr. Bear Squash-You-All-Flat tries squashing that and bounces way up into the sky and comes down so hard he hurts his back and never again tries to squash anything flat.

I read the book to Cannon while Elaine plays in the water with him. Cannon laughs softly at the right places in the story. Elaine tells me to reach in the linen closet and find the biggest towel we have. "He's starting to shiver a little," she says. I hand her the towel and she asks Cannon if he would like some nice hot soup. Cannon shrugs and Elaine tells me to go into the kitchen and heat up a can of chicken noodle soup.

In the kitchen, the sun isn't on the table any longer. Outside, a few big clouds have covered it for now, and there is no sign of the mailman. Then I see Mrs. Randall from next door walking along the sidewalk in front of our house. Elaine asks sometimes if I don't think Mrs. Randall will come over one day and find us upstairs while Cannon is outside playing by himself. I step back farther into the kitchen to make sure Mrs. Randall won't see me watching her. She is a good friend of my mother, and two of her sons are the same ages as Lisa and Brian. When she starts up our walkway, I feel my heart start to beat faster, even though we aren't doing anything except taking care of Cannon. I wait until she knocks on the door before I start toward it.

Mrs. Randall looks very nervous to me. "Alex," she says, stepping inside, "do you have the television on? Or the radio?"

I tell her no, and that Cannon seems to have a fever and we are taking care of him.

"Something terrible has happened," she says, and I wonder how she can know more about Cannon than we do when she has been in her house and we have been taking care of him. "President Kennedy has been shot in the head, did you know that?" She starts to cry then. Mrs. Randall walks up to me and puts her arms around me and her head on my shoulder. I lift my arms to fit around her back, thinking of Elaine holding Cannon the same way.

"What's wrong?" Elaine says. She has walked up behind Mrs. Randall and me, carrying Cannon in the big beach towel I gave her. The towel is wrapped around Cannon so fully that all you can see is a small part of his face.

"President Kennedy has been shot," Mrs. Randall says, moving away from me to talk to Elaine.

Elaine sits down on the couch with Cannon and I turn on the television. Mrs. Randall sits down next to Elaine and Cannon. "I think they'll close the schools right away," she says to me. "I think your mother will be home soon." She looks at Elaine and Cannon and then asks Cannon if he is okay. Cannon tells her he fell off the chair. Mrs. Randall holds Cannon's forehead and asks if we have a thermometer. I tell her we couldn't find it at the same moment that Elaine tells her he just had a cool bath to bring the fever down. It is also the same moment that the television picture comes on with Walter Cronkite looking like he is almost crying as he talks about the president.

"I'll be right back," Mrs. Randall says, and goes out the door.

"This is horrible," Elaine says.

"The president?" I say.

"Yes," she says with just the slightest impatience. "Somebody shot the president."

"I know," I say. "He was great."

Cannon, inside his towel, is resting on Elaine's shoulder. "You want to lie down in your bed, honey?" she coos into the side of the towel.

"What happened on television?" he says.

"They shot the president," I tell him.

Mrs. Randall comes back in without knocking. She is shaking a thermometer, and then brings it to Cannon's mouth. "Has he had any medicine?" she says to Elaine, and Elaine tells her yes.

"That's good," Mrs. Randall says. She pats at Cannon's towel. "I guess by the time the buses get going, it will be an hour before the kids get home from school," she says. "And Lord knows if they'll even let Ken off early. It's just terrible," she says. "I'll be glad when everyone is home and safe."

"You want to just stay here until people come home?" Elaine says to Mrs. Randall. I am surprised to hear her say that when she is usually afraid Mrs. Randall might come over.

"I could help a little with Cannon maybe," Mrs. Randall says, and reaches for the thermometer. She looks younger than she is, or afraid. "Until his mom gets here."

"How is it?" I say, nodding at the thermometer.

She rolls the thermometer in her fingers to be able to read it. "Not too bad," she says. "Just over a hundred and one. I think the cooling bath was just the thing," she says toward Elaine.

Outside, the clouds keep moving across the sun and then away again. On the television, they are showing a long line of open-top cars in Dallas, Texas, and talking about the president being shot and that he may not live. Elaine pulls Cannon's head to her shoulder again, as if he shouldn't see. Mrs. Randall gets up for a moment to look out the window toward her house. I sit at one end of the couch, waiting for my mother to come home, wondering if it is because of Cannon or the president that I am working so hard not to cry. After a few moments, while we all watch, Elaine asks me if I ever started the soup for Cannon.

A Short History of the Stamps

For the house he purchased just after World War II—"$4,000 cash, I've never had a mortgage," he'll tell you today—my father bought a long brown couch with a big compartment under the seat. The couch, which my boyhood eye remembers as twelve feet long, opened up in the manner of a stupendously long mouth. You grabbed the front just above the floor and lifted, and there appeared a space as long as the couch, three feet back and a foot deep. The couch had been in the house five or six years before I became aware of it as other than something to climb on. And when I did—when I became old enough to react with wonder at its opening—I was told that I shouldn't ever open it.

"It's Edwin's storage space, Alex," my mother told me when she found me straining to lift it as I'd seen my father do. "He keeps his old papers in there." Because my mother called him Edwin every time she spoke of him or to him, I did as well, and do today, when he is an old man and I am well into middle age. Since I was forbidden entry into Edwin's couch—nearly half a century ago—I tried all the harder to lift it open, and succeeded for the first time when I was perhaps eight, and my parents were in the back yard talking to neighbors.

Inside were more envelopes and pieces of envelopes than I had any idea existed in the whole world. This, I was to understand later, was where Edwin stored the stamps he had not yet soaked from the envelopes or envelope fragments or postcards, and then mounted in his collection books. He owned, my mother told me, every U.S. stamp since the year of his birth except one—a stamp with a zeppelin on it from the teens or twenties that his own mother had not let him buy as a boy. The envelopes and square cuts of paper formed a mild mound shape the first time I saw them in the couch, as if he had tossed each one in toward the center and it had settled softly onto the pile.

By the time I was old enough to understand the significance of the stamps and their role in my father's life—"Yes, you wrote me a letter and that's appreciated, but you know better than to not use a commemorative"—the couch mouth had been filled, and he was using most of two small filing cabinets for the same purpose. My impression, at age fourteen or fifteen, was that my father was wasting his collection, not keeping up with it.

"Oh no," he said when I asked him. "I've mounted lots of them. I'll show you." He went to the room he used for an office—a room so full and piled with papers that it made you think about the card catalogue at the main library being dumped out and then a fan being turned on—and came back with a stack of pretty black binders. Inside were pages of stamps mounted so precisely as to look like a museum.

"See," Edwin said, "these are the hinges." He used the front edge of a fingernail to tip a stamp up from the bottom, to show me how each stamp was affixed to the page with a tiny piece of nearly clear, very thin paper that kept even the back of the stamp from direct contact with the page.

"Wow," I said, and soon my father was telling me detailed stories about the individual stamps in the books—about misprints and commemorations of events, about the rise in postal rates over the years, and about the stamp his mother hadn't let him buy.

"Today that stamp costs hundreds of dollars. Back then I could have had it for two or three dollars."

We looked at the stamps until he must have sensed my interest waning.

"Well," he said loudly, as if to conclude. "Just remember that you mustn't go into the couch." I felt a sinking through my body as he said this. It was as if I were eight again, and he had caught me trying to lift up the big couch-mouth to get to his stamps.

"Sure," I said, shrugging. "I know that."

He carried the albums back to his office room with a body language that indicated I was not to follow and find out where he kept them.

Within two years after that day, my father bought my mother her own house, in the same neighborhood we'd always lived in. Once again he paid cash, though he'd never held anything but modest-paying jobs. ("I saved," he'll tell you, "I saved until I was twenty-eight before I married.") I did not know why they were going to live in different houses, and did not learn until months later that it had to do with a woman from Norway who lived nearby and with whom my father had taken up with off and on for many years, always then returning to profess love for my mother and always, until she'd demanded her own house, resulting in her taking him back. I do not remember if my brothers and sister and I were told we'd live with my mother rather than with Edwin, or whether it was the natural sequence of things, but I do remember that within a few months after my father began living by himself, the whole house over on Oak Drive took on the appearance of the office room he'd had. In the living room were stacks of mail and newspapers, piles of books and pieces of lumber, a blanket in a little pile here, an old typewriter case over there. In the kitchen, the sink and counters overflowed with dishes and pots and food containers, as if Edwin were a little boy, unable to keep up with the demands of a house. Cannon, the youngest son, who carried his father's name under his nickname, visited him most often, delivering stamps he'd clipped from letters at the other house.

On the relatively rare times when I went to see him, he often came to the door or even stepped outside, as if ashamed of the disarray inside. "How are you?" he would call out too loudly, seeming to have to affect his joy at seeing me because of his dismay over his house. His conversation topics, if I had nothing to talk about, moved among three things—what my mother was doing these days, how I was doing in school, and if he could persuade anyone beyond Cannon to save stamps for him.

"Oh, you bet," I'd tell him each time, and make a promise to myself to look at the mail more closely and cut the stamps for him. I do not recall that I ever did follow through, leaving it to Cannon. In later years my mother would resume the practice, but at this time the woman from Norway was too close at hand for her to have much to do with him at all. Sometimes when I was out in the neighborhood, I would see Edwin and the Norwegian woman walking. In our neighborhood it was still a scandal to see them together. Her husband had moved somewhere out of the neighborhood. Her three sons had stayed behind with her, and so even if there were any temptation for Edwin and Erica to live together, the presence of her boys must have blocked it. I wondered once when I saw them walking near the baseball field if she got stamps from Norway for him.

When Edwin and Erica were free of all their children — all had reached adulthood except Cannon, who had drowned when he came out of a canoe on the Potomac River — they did move into a house together, though they did not marry. The house was on the other side of town from our neighborhood, and though my father spent most of his time there, he did not give up his house on Oak Drive. The house became part of neighborhood legend. Brian, who has lived all his life in that neighborhood where we grew up, was approached by young children during those years, who asked if Brian's father really did have every newspaper ever printed in there, if he really did come back in the middle of the night every Saturday to check on things. Through love or embarrassment or both, Brian defended his father through those years, telling people that Edwin planned to get the property back in shape the next summer, that he still needed time to recover from the tragic loss of a son. Summers passed, and the house took on an ever more eerie appearance. The paint peeled off the trim, broken windows were left unrepaired or were covered with pieces of wood. The yard grew all season without mowing or weeding, and the low brick wall my father started constructing years before sat trailing off into sloped yard, with loose bricks, untouched for years, being slowly integrated into the weeds and soil.

Now that my brother and sister and I lived well away from Edwin, he became even more interested in us as providers of stamps. You could write him about getting a new job and moving to a new apartment, and in his letter back, the first thing he would write about was what kind of stamp you had put on the envelope and if you had put it on at an angle to assure that the cancellation did not obliterate parts of the face of the stamp. Lisa, by then living a tortured life in New York State, wrote rarely and often incoherently. When you went to visit him where he lived with Erica the Norwegian, you could see that she was stricter with him about his clutter than my mother had been. There was one room in the small house where she had a sewing machine and an exercise bicycle, and on the other side of the room was a large old desk that was piled high with the Edwin stacks, as she called them. She teased about his clutter and about the house he still kept on the other side of town. "One day it will fall in upon itself and then they will bulldoze the lot and begin all over again," she said with her slight accent, and Edwin would squirm and say yes, he was going to get to it, that he needed to get it cleaned out.

"How are all those stamps in there?" my brother asked Edwin one Thanksgiving. "Aren't they going to get destroyed?"

"Yes, yes," my father said with impatience, for his shame over the state of his house was so strong that it overwhelmed any perception he might have had of my brother's concern for the collection. "And I've gotten a great deal of that stuff out of there, you know. I need to do more." He would then work to change the subject.

Over the next few years, as Brian bought a house in the old neighborhood and became an officer in the community improvement organization, he took more and more interest in the old house. I wondered if he had been made an officer because people felt they'd then have a better chance to have him do something about the rotting eyesore at 38 Oak Drive. And at some point, whether out of civic pride or love for his father, Brian took charge of the long-awaited house-emptying project. He convinced my father to meet him there every afternoon at 5:30 for the whole of one summer, and they worked at getting everything that Edwin wanted out of the old house, so it could be sold.

Inside, floorboards had rotted through, the ceiling sagged or hung loose in spots. Mouse and bird droppings dotted or covered stacks of papers. There was no longer any running water in the house, as the pipes had long since frozen and burst. And in one corner of the living room, with its back against an unscarred wall as if to try to edge away from the decay and chaos before it, was the old brown couch. It was faded to a much lighter color than it had been back when Brian and I were boys, and in spots it was water-stained and torn and eaten-away by insects or rodents. Brian told me that he and Edwin avoided it for weeks as they cleaned and discarded, as they advanced the house to a point where it could be put on the market as a fixer-upper. Then, when the couch's presence seemed to assert itself to the point that it could no longer be ignored, they approached it together, or so Brian told me.

"You do the honors," Edwin said, gesturing toward the couch.

"Me?" Brian said. "Me open the couch none of us could ever touch?"

"Indeed," Edwin said. "Let's take a look. Open 'er up."

My brother reported that Edwin sat immediately down and put his head in his hands when they looked inside. At one end of the pile, insects had transformed the envelopes into what appeared at first glance to be a big pile of brown rice, with no sign of any individual envelope or stamp. All of the colors of the stamps and the envelopes had been digested into one light-brown mass of tiny bits.

The work had been carried out about a third of the way across the expanse of envelopes. There was a narrow section of transition between the devoured remains and the yellowed, delicate envelopes and cuttings that were still there, but there were no immediately visible insects, as if work had been halted for some reason. Brian sought to comfort and reassure his father, to tell him that there was still a lot to be salvaged. But Edwin was apparently unconsolable just then, and got in his car and drove home to the woman from Norway. My brother called me for advice, and while I had none, we decided that the remains in the couch should be salvaged. Brian went to the grocery store for cardboard boxes, reported back to the house on Oak Drive, and then used a snow shovel to scoop the contents of the old couch into the boxes. He said he had to fight his own tears, not so much because of the state of ruin itself as for the feeling of a man's dreams—alive since his boyhood—having been neglected and forgotten so long. Brian said he and Edwin had found stacks of unclipped envelopes all over the house, that between the old filing cabinets and the piles in the house, he and Edwin had filled fifty-two cardboard boxes with stamp materials.

"He apparently had everybody at the school—all the other teachers—saving stamps for him for all those years," Brian said. "And that's not counting the stuff in the couch. Or the boxes we found that he had brought from his mother's house when he and Mom moved in here before we were born. There were maybe two dozen of those in the attic, and most of them in pretty good shape, amazingly enough. A lot of them had been taped shut and on some of them the tape had held and no critters went in. He broke down once up there too, when he told me that Mom taped those boxes for him, thirty years ago or something."

Brian said that after the cleanup had been completed, he had taken it upon himself to store the boxes of stamps, and then had gotten permission from Edwin to do that, but just temporarily. "I need to go through them," my father told Brian with no sense of irony.

"He could have been a great man," Brian told me on the phone a few days later, a bit overcome. "All that energy and drive and knowledge. He just never could get it harnessed."

"Too many women problems getting in the way," I offered.

"Maybe so," Brian said. "Maybe too many stamps."

Over the next few years, the woman from Norway became seriously ill, and the house she shared with my father began to take on the look of the old house on Oak. As she became less and less mobile and moved toward the painful death that cancer would bring her, she asserted less control over the house. Small piles of envelopes here and there gave way to full corners of rooms piled high with magazines and newspapers and car parts and electronic gear, as my father's own form of cancer advanced upon another house.

At this point, Brian suggested to me that we give my father the ultimate Christmas present. That we take the garage at the house where he and the Norwegian woman lived and transform it into a secure, climate-controlled space for the stamps, and then take it upon ourselves to scour all the rooms of that house, find all the stamps there and then get the scores of boxes that Brian still had in storage, and put them all in the garage so that Edwin would have all his stamps in one place, so that he could walk out there and work on them any time he wanted.

"And the albums too," he said. "Get everything in there in one place."

"If he still has them," I said.

"Oh, he has at least some of them," Brian said. "I've seen them."

And so we pooled our money and hired a friend of Brian's to install the climate system and the humidity controlling devices and the fluorescent lights, and we changed an everyday garage that had been full of old bicycles and strollers and lawn mowers and yard tools into a concrete-floored, wall-boarded space with securely locking windows, a whole wall of shelving and, beneath the larger window, a twelve-foot long work table. Brian, long the most wary of Edwin's ability to take hold of the collection, became the cheerleader as we worked. For every doubt I expressed, he had a vision of his father's dreams realized. Edwin was of course aware as we worked, but he seemed content to be distracted by Erica's failing health, and abandoned his usual need to know and understand everything, and instead allowed his children to proceed with whatever it was they were doing. Erica was at this point in the hospital, and probably knew nothing of the changes we were making to their property.

It was at least in part because of Erica's impending death that the Christmas gift we created for my father was not received with the same spirit in which it had been created. That, and my father's own reserved and careful personality. He did tour it with us, and refrained from the questions about materials choices and construction techniques and costs that he would have asked under more normal circumstances.

"It's great to have all of the stamps in here," he said

in the end, and then could not resist remembering to mention to me that my last letter, which I'd mailed from a grocery store on lunch hour to make sure he got it to know my plans for Christmas travel, had had an unacceptable stamp on it. "You know I can't stand those flag stamps," he said. "There are two or three new commemoratives out just this week, you know."

Brian, who had walked tentatively behind us as we conducted our tour, came suddenly forward. I could feel his presence before he spoke.

"Jesus H. Fucking Christ," he said measuredly, and not without a hint of irony borne of using a phrase that none of us would, at least in the presence of any of the rest of us. "Here we are in a damned air-conditioned, climate-controlled, perfectly ventilated, totally queer-for-stamps room, built for you by your children, *and* it's Christmas, *and* you've been provided a chance to salvage one huge broken chunk of your life and maybe your psyche in the meantime, and you are asking Alex about a damn *flag stamp*? When he just handed you the potential to save every fucking stamp you own? Is that what I just heard?"

Brian turned then, threw his arms out briefly in disbelieving disgust, walked out of the new room, got into his car and drove away. We stood in silence a moment, Edwin and I. I found no capacity to meet his glance. The space we stood in felt suddenly cold, the way new rooms with concrete floors often do.

"Well," Edwin said finally, "another Christmas that we didn't quite pull off right." He sat down then, in the old chair from his office on Oak Drive. "That *I* didn't pull off right." He put his head in his hands.

My father no longer lives on the property where the stamps garage is. Four years after Erica died, not long before Lisa died, he met a woman on a hike along the canal west of town, and perhaps a year after that, he moved into her house, not far from a city about fifty miles from the one where we grew up. The process of selling the house he and Erica had lived in was much more quickly expedited than the sale of the house on Oak Drive, simply because Edwin had very little to do with it. One of Erica's sons ran a commercial real estate company, and had at his immediate access the legal and accounting connections to push the sale along. My father ranted and raved early on about being railroaded, and when things were finally accomplished, he was angry enough to say that he'd never set foot on the property again, even though the resolution of the dispute had taken a significant chunk of his share to cover his continued ownership of the stamps garage and the resulting "severe diminution of the value of the property by virtue of the severing of the outbuilding portion of the property and grounds, from the estate as a whole," as the final papers read.

"Who wrote this garbage?" Edwin said. "Not only are these lawyers crooks, they have no inkling at all of the English language."

In the house where Edwin and his companion of nearly ten years now live, the signs are clear. The house is not big, and Jeanne—she is a large, strong-willed woman who is the daughter of parents born in Greece—maintains the one spare room as her office. So Edwin's collections and stacks are not in the house at all. They are outside, at the head of the driveway, where there is a building not much larger than a shed. Here, amid garden tools and other implements, is a space for my father's stamps. It is after all her house they live in, and so my father sheepishly follows her order—"it's certainly her prerogative"—and carries his little pile of envelopes and fragments out the kitchen door and down the steps to the little shed and its single hanging bulb.

Though he has relented a time or two on his long-ago vow and driven to the stamps garage for brief visits, he has never set aside a period of days or even hours to go in there and undertake the work that has been a goal for all his life and that he still says he will accomplish, even though it is now more than seventy years since he began collecting, and through all of that time, he has apparently never moved past the stamps from 1931 in his books of mounted stamps. It is my brother's opinion that it is at least thirty years since he has mounted a stamp at all, and it has now been almost fifteen years since Brian and his father have exchanged more than polite niceties and necessaries with each other.

Jeanne talks to me—for Brian will no longer discuss the topic—about how to get Edwin to work on the stamps, and I, a middle-aged son of an old old man, can only shrug and smile and appreciate her care for him. But in the next moment she will grow testy with him for leaving pieces of mail around the house, and send him outside to do his business in the shed. Out there now, sharing space on a shelf with a case of motor oil and two old photograph frames, are three shoeboxes full of envelopes and pieces of envelopes, waiting to be clipped and soaked and mounted in the books that sit with the other boxes of envelopes, fifty miles down the road, in a squarish, concrete-floored building on which my father stopped paying the utilities eight years ago this month.

Kentucky Moon

Alice sat where she sat every afternoon, on the most-trod part of the single wooden step in front of the cabin, facing out into the yard. The yard, the step, the cabin and the quick rise of the mountain behind them were in eastern Kentucky, near the start of another century.

"Alice, come in here for the kitchen chores," her mother called to her, from back inside.

"I'm waiting for Daddy," Alice said matter-of-factly, counting on her mother to turn to the fire or the soup, or something else.

"There's sweeping and there are ashes," her mother called.

Alice said nothing, sitting still on the step, where the wood beneath her was so foot-worn that when you sat on it, it felt softer than wood, almost warm.

Then her mother's voice was closer: "I told you there's sweeping and ashes."

Alice hunched her body down and forward, pulling her shoulders in toward her chin. "They'll be there just after Daddy gets here too," she said toward her lap.

Her mother came down one side of the step and squatted in front of Alice. She put her curled forefinger at the base of Alice's chin and pulled it up with gentle force, which Alice did not resist. "You want me to tell your daddy you talked that way to your mother?" she said.

Alice squinted her eyes as if an unnatural light were coming from the face she'd been pulled up to look into. "I didn't mean anything smart," she said quietly, with too much poise for her years. "He will be along in a minute and then I will sweep and take out the ashes, Momma." She said "momma" softly, touching it with apology and plea.

Her mother stood then, with a sigh and a wave of her arms and then an impatient expelling of breath as she went back up the one step and into the house.

Alice Kell was six years old the day she sat on the steps more than a hundred years ago. She was a girl who watched her daddy the way her brother watched a cricket to learn its jumps so he could catch it out of the air; the way her big sister watched every boy her own age or older, looking for the husband she turned desperate for the day she turned thirteen. Their daddy, Perris Kell, was forty-one and barely five feet tall. When you came up on him from behind across the field to the side of the house, you could think he was one of the boys from school. From the front you could see how the coal dust had darkened his face to a Kentucky-mountain tan, how tobacco smoke had turned his crooked teeth yellow as corn. Little shoulders he had—far smaller than Alice's mother's— set back hard and straight in the same shirts Alice's brother wore, buttoned sometimes to the top as if to square himself off against the world he went into every day.

Alice Kell saw the place where she lived with big eyes, with an involuntary sort of knowledge packed up high in her little chest—stacked there all tight and moving toward formation, like new coal. She stored her feelings about the mountains alongside the deep, aching, equally involuntary love she had for her father. Who else knew that underneath his hard worn face, he was as fragile as the skeleton that hung at the back of the schoolroom? Who else knew—without ever being told—that the little man down in the mine was assigned things to do and places to reach and crawl that no one else got, just because of his size? Who else knew that her daddy did them all without ever a word of question or complaint?

Alice knew all that, and came home every day from school to wait for him to come home so she could be sure he had come safely out of the mountain one more day. It began to get dark in the hollow by four o'clock in the summer and three in the winter, adding to the feel of danger about the mountains. They encircled Alice and her family day and night, and swallowed Perris every day for ten or twelve hours. The times the mountains felt safest were when the big full moon was right above the cabin, right in the middle of a clear sky, shining down brighter than the light they had inside. On a clear night it shone down on them like magic, moving too quickly across the little cut of sky above the hollow.

What Alice didn't know, and what her mother didn't know either, on these afternoons out front when the dark and cold filled the hollow, was that she and her mother were building something between them over Perris Kell. His wife was getting bigger by the year, and as she did, Perris must have seemed smaller to her, somehow less a man, with those feelings building on some level as deep as an undiscovered vein in the mountain. Alice could look at her mother sometimes with eyes that put a look of something like fear in her mother's face. You could not be jealous of your own six-year-old daughter, and Polly Kell was not. And when you were six, you could not know the way your mother loved your daddy, and Alice Kell did not. But every time mother and daughter met hard on the soft step out front or at the corner of the kitchen table—every time Polly had to punish Alice or Alice got those eyes at her mother—Perris was right there in the middle even if he was seven miles away and a hundred feet underground.

Once, deep in that winter when Alice was six and the shaft gave way and four men died and Perris took on a gimp leg for the rest of his life—once in that winter and three days before the accident—Alice, not knowing it would come out of her mouth, said to her mother: "Do you think Perris is safer in the mine than he is here when you are in a spell like you are now?" Her mother's face filled here and there with splotchy, purplish red before her hand came at Alice's left cheek—hard and flat and with enough force to make Alice fall over to one side. But not cry. *Perris*, Alice had called him, and had asked a question she had not known existed before she spoke it. His name had hung right there between them for a few seconds before she was slapped, as if she had never heard it before, as if it had never before been spoken. Little Perris Kell was her daddy.

When they broke the school into two parts the fall that Alice was thirteen, there were all of a sudden three times as many girls as boys in the older students' part. Some of the girls whispered to each other that their husband chances had shrunk down to all-but-gone-away because of that. Alice listened but did not tell them how foolish that was. In school the previous year, the boys who had made the numbers nearly equal were all younger than the whisperers. And the older boys who had left would have gone to the mines whether the school had been changed or not.

If you asked Alice about a husband, which no one did, she'd say yes, she wanted one. But not the first one that presented himself and not one-third as bad as her sister had at the same age, nor one-half as bad as the girls in the school who could feel the field shrinking even when it wasn't. Alice's sister lived in Middlesboro now, and wrote letters home about nothing but the weather and laundry and sidewalks along the street and in every third one that Jim was doing just fine. No one said out loud that Eileen sounded lonesome. Alice's mother read the letters and each time talked about how far it was to Middlesboro.

Perris Kell had a different job at the company now, and almost never went into the mine. He still came home black-dusted and tired and hunched-over and small and limping, but at work he stayed up near the rail cars, weighing or inspecting or getting things planned to be on time. Alice still watched, but she didn't watch as hard as she used to or as hard as the girls did for husbands. She was calm and patient, watching what was before her from her mother and father, from her sister in the big city and her brother—bigger than his daddy and maybe smarter and slightly less dear to Alice, and already in the mine. Her family was suspended safely for a time, it seemed to her, and so there was no call for urgency in her own life. She was the best student at the school when she chose to be, which was nearly always, and she did not often disagree with her mother, because her mother would be the next one to have a change in her life, whatever it might be. Perris seemed to know it too, soft as he was with his wife when she hit a week or two spell.

It was within that year that Polly Kell died. Alice went to the room where Polly and Perris slept because it was after nine and Polly had not come into the kitchen. Polly was in the bed—a big mound under the covers taking up so much room it was hard to see where Perris would fit when he was there too.

"Momma?" Alice said, tentatively—at the door, her eyes getting bigger.

"Momma?" once again, and then she went in, feeling somehow like the mother instead of the daughter. With no one else in the house, she walked back out of the bedroom, pulled the door closed behind her and went back through the kitchen, out the front, down the worn step and on her way to walk to town and the coal tipple, where Perris would be. He would know where Roy was and would go find him, and would ask Alice to send the telegram to Eileen in Middlesboro.

Alice's daddy turned into a different, fuller man the day his wife died, and Alice saw it begin the second she told him. He came gently to her, put his short arm around her shoulder to pull her to him. He thanked her for walking the seven miles when he would have been home in just a little over an hour. He said he was going to find Roy, and then told her the things she knew he would. "She just got too big," Perris said to Alice as he turned to go. "She couldn't seem to stop herself. She was running away from life itself." There was a look of open love in his face as he spoke—for Polly, for Alice, for the rest of his family. He was calm, matter-of-fact and a little straighter as he stood.

The family's mourning was equally calm and straightforward. They buried Polly Nelson Kell with just seven people other than the family there to witness, and then they went back home to the cabin in the hollow and took up their lives where they'd left them. In the corner of the main room was a chair that no one sat in— Polly's chair—and it slowly filled with things they put in it. A sweater, Polly's shoes, a bonnet she'd not worn for many years, her Bible.

Alice went back, for only a few days, to watching out more closely for Perris, to noting when he arose and how he looked at his food and what expression his face carried when he came home from work. But she didn't do it long, because he didn't need it long. Perris went back and forth to work and he talked more to his family and took over the writing of the letters to Middlesboro. He smiled more often and he soon weighed just a little more, as if he might have eaten less when Polly was around, maybe with the hope that she'd do the same. He was a widower of the type that looks inward and to his kin instead of back out into the world to try again with a wife. That part of his life had been put in a box and lowered into the ground. It was covered then, and put away, like something stored away in the attic when it was no longer needed.

The man Alice met turned twenty-two years old a few weeks after she turned nineteen. He was a smallish man, though not as small as Perris. She met him near the tipple on the only day in her life she went that way from town toward home for no reason but to go that way. She wondered as she walked if there were something happening with Perris to make her go that way. Or Roy. It was Saturday afternoon and neither one of them was even in town. She looked up at the pure blue sky and decided it was why she was going that way. The train slowed just as she neared the tipple, and from between coal cars a man hopped down. He was wearing strange, billowy pants and long, tight white socks. When he had stopped running with the motion that the train had sent him to the ground with, he was next to Alice. He was carrying a small black satchel, smaller than a doctor's bag.

"This isn't Herrod, is it?" he said.

"The town?" Alice said.

"Right, the town."

"No, it's not," she said, deciding to give him no further information. How could you get off a train and miss the town you were in by two towns?

"It is that way?" he said, pointing in the direction the train was heading.

"It is," Alice said.

"Well, I thank you ma'am," he said, and tipped the silly cap on his head at her, as if with irony.

They walked side by side as the train moved just slightly faster than they were walking, while she thought about him tipping the cap. "You're not walking there," she said, halfway between a question and telling him so.

"No, I'm not," he said. "Once the train starts rolling a little faster again, I'll hop back on, if I don't get caught and shooed off."

"Shooed off?" she said. "Who'd shoo you off?" And what kind of man said "shoo"?

"Railway officials," he said. "Coal company people." His face opened up a little as he said this, to where, when she decided to look into the face, she could see big eyes and a small, easy smile.

"You're hopping the train?" she said. She looked at him again, thinking about coal dust blowing on him from the cars.

"I'm due in Herrod for a game before you know it," he said.

"A game?" she said.

"Baseball," he said. He raised the bag up slightly in her direction, as if in explanation.

She took three more steps beside him. "Where's the rest of the team?" she said.

"All there, I imagine," he said. "I wasn't able to leave till mid-morning, and so here I am." He stopped walking then, and she did the same.

"My name is Daniel Coggins," he said, "and I'm from just over the Virginia line."

Alice said her name and extended her hand to the man who'd jumped off the train right next to her on the day she'd walked through town and along the tracks. The first time in her life she'd offered her hand to someone. And in a few minutes, after they'd resumed walking, when the train began to roll again, Daniel Coggins jumped up between two cars while the train was moving slowly enough that it was still easy to do. He stood between two cars and began to wave. Alice raised her hand to wave back and then felt her feet move a little faster, as if to stay even with the slow-moving train that called for no more speed than walking. She stayed even with where he stood, looking at him and then at the wheels. She was not sure who reached first. He pulled her up with a slow, strong, easy motion, took her tiny waist between his hands for the part of a second it took to steady her as she came up, and she was on her way to watch a baseball game in Herrod, just into the next county, two towns down the tracks from the town she'd never left in her life except for the one trip to Middlesboro to visit Eileen.

Two men who don't talk much wouldn't fight over holding a baby—grandbaby to one and daughter to the other—if they wanted to, for the simple reason that neither would want to allow any chance for the other to call him a sissy. A pretty granddaughter she was, born four years to the month after Alice Kell married Daniel Coggins, which happened one month and twelve days after they rode away on a train and Alice came back home late in the evening, in an automobile filled with men. She got out of the car with her head hung, but picked it up before she was five feet from the car. She turned and waved to the men about to drive away, and then she went up the one step into the cabin and went to knock on Perris's door.

"Daddy?" she said, quietly.

He answered her right away, as she knew he would. She knew he would never have gotten up to scold her or even to check on her beyond what he could hear as she came in, but he listened when spoken to, spoke when he had something to say, and on this night arose without protest when he was asked to.

"I know what you think," Alice began, and then she righted herself again as she had in the yard. "Well, I don't know what you think. But I am going to tell you all about where I was and what I did and then I will know what you think and what I think too." And as she began, Perris leaned back, as if he knew it would be truth he heard, and that it would not hurt him.

"I know a little about stealing second three times in one game," was the first thing he said back to her, "but I don't know a thing about love at first sight. I have heard of it, I have heard people swear up and down it's real and true and even lasting, but I have never seen it up close and real the way you can see a fellow steal second base." He grinned at her then, letting her know he liked what he heard of the baseball player who snuck away on the train to play, letting her know he wasn't the one to stand in the way of her understanding of how love was going to work for her.

The little girl was named Grace. She was small and beautiful. Perris said she looked like Daniel. Daniel said she looked like Perris, at least what he must have looked like before his face turned into an old prune. They laughed, getting as close as they could to being sissies for just a moment. In truth Grace looked more like her mother than anyone else, with a tiny mouth and a short nose turned up even more than usual on babies.

Alice had no choice about moving to Virginia. Not because Daniel demanded it—because he didn't—but because it was what he wanted and where he worked and where they would live. Alice knew when she didn't like something she could feel it somewhere in her. She didn't feel anything close to that when they talked about moving to Wythe County. Alice thought of Perris, and of her sister living in Middlesboro and Roy not married and Perris not having any kind of woman around him at all. But it was fleeting and then gone. She told Perris it was really only a few counties away, but as much as he had traveled in his life, telling him about something in another state was not much different than talking about Paris.

The visit when the two men went all sweet over Grace was when she was less than three months old. The next visit, for minor reasons that piled upon one another—a missed train, bad weather, illness and a death—was not until Grace was six. This time Daniel and Alice traveled in a car back to her home. The trip, across the seven counties, would take most of a day. Grace was excited at the start, then sick, then sleepy, then unhappy. Alice, carrying her second child, worried every mile how little Grace was holding up with the journey, about how many flats would have to be fixed, about a drive through the mountains in December. It was when Grace was asleep on Alice's lap that Daniel crested a hill at the Kentucky border, went into the shade and had no chance to see the ice that had formed from the mountain-side spring that leaked onto the road and froze when the sun did not hit the packed-mud road surface. The car slid toward the shoulder as if in slow motion, as Alice felt all her organs drop within her. She tried to hold Grace, but when the car hit the ditch at the side of the roadway, it halted abruptly, as little Grace was thrown out of her arms and both of them went violently forward, with Alice's impact broken some by the physical presence of her daughter before her. Grace screamed and brought her hands to her face once the car was stopped, blood coming through her little fingers as Alice matched her scream, looking at Daniel both to see how his face looked at the horror before him, and then to see if he was hurt. He was not, and within days, the task before them was to try to count themselves lucky that no more had happened to their perfect, beautiful child than that she had lost her right eye. She was brave and uncomplaining while the wound itself healed, and quickly more at ease with her glass eye than her parents. Back home, after two months, Alice told Daniel she would never ride in a car again, and hoped he wouldn't either. He put his arms around her easily, almost as if he knew she would hold to her vow for all the years until Grace was grown and had moved away to Maryland.

What Alice wanted to see with Grace was what she could still see as plain as the day before her from her own life: the night she'd come home from riding the train with Daniel and sat down to talk to her daddy about how and what love was going to mean to her. Grace, pretty, twenty-one and back home for a visit, was talking to her mother about a man she'd met.

"I'm afraid he might be close to forty," she said. "I mean he's going bald anyway. He's so careful, sort of, so aware of every single thing." What Alice knew then was that this was the man Grace would marry.

"You don't want to marry an old man," Alice said as

soon as that thought occurred to her, and knowing she shouldn't, knowing to lean back and watch and hope for the best for her daughter.

"Well, I really don't know his age," Grace said, looking askance at her mother. "But I will find out the next time I see him, which might well be sooner than I thought if you're going to tell me what to do the way you always do."

"Where's he from?" Alice said.

"Up there," Grace said. "In Baltimore. He works the same place I do. He's a nice man."

"Born in Baltimore?"

"No, Momma, he was born on Mars in 1513," Grace said, and turned away. "I really just met him and I like him a lot, so I told you about him," she said back over her shoulder. "That was a mistake. I don't know where he was born."

"No, no," Alice called softly, knowing Grace was right, gritting her teeth at her own inability to hold and act on what she knew about how to treat people, to back away when it was time to back away and speak when it was time to speak. All her life she had known when and how to do that, had known when people were foolish and when to let them go ahead and find it out, had understood the people who were her family. But with her oldest daughter, so vulnerable from the day she was born, her face broken before she even went to school, she had never been able to act from any context other than fear of hurt, of injury or slight to this precious girl.

Grace left the next day, and Alice told Daniel she was going to take a job. She had talked about it for several years as Grace and her two sisters got older, but now she said she was going to do it. Going to go work in the Barnes & Gilley store, in the fabric and patterns department. She had fallen in love years earlier with the bolts of fabric that came into the store on big trucks, had been amazed at the quantity of fabric that was sitting there for the buying in the little town where they lived. And so, as she entered middle age, Alice aimed some of the focus of her life into the department store, as if to build a shield against some of the pain with Grace, as if to force herself away from her naked love for Grace and the other two, which lived always inside her almost like an illness, and to which Grace responded with a shrug at the best moments and a near-mocking coldness at worst.

It was during this time—on a summer day after Alice had mailed him a letter—that Perris Kell died. He was eighty-one—an old old man for a coal miner—and the last time she'd seen him he'd still been thin and strong-looking, but with a face so darkened and cut so deep with lines as to make young children take a step back when they saw him for the first time. Alice had not seen him since the summer, when she had gone back home— with Daniel—because Perris wrote he wanted them to come get some things out of the house before it was too late for it to be clear who was to get what. Alice wrote back that she would not hear any of that, but that she would come to see him. She knew when she saw him that he had indeed told them to come because he knew he was going to die. He was calm and easy, clear-eyed. He took Alice and Daniel to the back of the cabin where Kells had lived for nearly a hundred years and soon would no more, and gave Daniel the tools he cherished most. "You use tools," Perris said to Daniel. "Roy loses them." He let a small, rueful smile cross his mouth just then, glancing at Alice, who was told to take all of the things from the kitchen except the few that Perris used day to day. "None of these things are fancy enough for

Eileen," he said "Take them home for your girls." Both times he spoke that way Alice wanted to protest, but did not. Perris had thought about what he wanted to happen and he had spoken, and it was to be respected.

The boy was named Alex, and in the summer when he was six, it occurred suddenly one day to Alice that a sort of unholy trio was formed. She had loved Daniel now for more than forty years; perhaps not as rashly as the day she had met him on the train, but among the things she liked best and told no one was growing old with him in a peaceful way. She'd been on the lookout for many years for signs of what happened between her own parents. Neither she nor Daniel gained much weight, and in all else, they seemed to stay in at least rough balance with one another. Spaces between them shifted and changed over the years, but he was the same polite, slightly diffident, sweet man he'd been the day he'd talked about getting shooed away from a train. And Alice told herself she had learned to love Grace all over again and in a new way after she had indeed married the strange man she met at work. He was from a place even worse than Mars: Germany.

Alice had disciplined herself the same way she did with housework or church work or any other part of her life; she spoke to herself about it for as long as it took for her to pull back from wanting to write Grace every day, to worry every day that Edwin would take advantage of her some way, that he was somehow tied to the horrible man who ran Germany. Alice worked to welcome whatever came her way in relation to Grace. And she had loved little Alex since the day she'd helped him be born. He was a quiet, cautious boy—too much like his father, she thought—at least until that spring when Daniel put him on stilts, not a week after he had his tonsils out.

Rendered much taller and at ease almost immediately with the stilts, Alex changed. Up there with his long wooden legs, he deepened his voice, he imitated Red Skelton and his own father. He tromped around the back yard—sticking holes in the lawn—and even up the steep hill to where the clotheslines and the strawberries were. Alice looked at Grace and saw no fear or hesitation at what the boy did, no fear of accident. Daniel taught Alex a new trick every day: baseball, fishing, a bicycle, a scooter, or the stilts Alex had cut and assembled himself, and Alex could not contain his pride at what he could do that he couldn't before this summer visit when his father had stayed back home in Baltimore.

So there was that shift in the house, a move of Daniel and Grace and Alex into one corner that was always moving, that was never without a plan about where it would go and what it would do next. Alice, never athletic, never inclined to fish or even go outside except to hang the laundry or weed the strawberries, felt herself more and more over in the other part of the room, or in one room of the house—with no one talking to her, no one asking her what she thought or what she might like to do. For the first time in her life, she was aware of a hollow feeling inside her, as if there was something she did not understand or that she was being left out of. It occurred to her one day that she was an orphan. And what did she have to do with Alex except to make him a plate of eggs at breakfast and remind him to wipe his feet and not let the screen door slam when he came into the house?

Alice told no one of her feelings, and fought them within herself. Who were these three but the people she loved the most? What was it inside her that made her want to stop them moving around so much, to slow down when they did move?

It was Alex who broke this spell, on a day out in the back yard where he had transformed, in the span of one summer, from a timid boy to a little imitation of his grandfather; a boy who woke up every morning with a plan of what he'd do with that day and then had to hurry through his breakfast to get to it, to get outside and taste the thrill of the newest new thing he'd learned. This was a late summer day under a perfectly blue sky, in the early afternoon, after Alex and Daniel had spent the morning down in the basement with the tools, then come upstairs for a quick lunch and gone right back down. Over the summer they had built toy boats and little benches, the stilts and new shelves for the tools that filled the old coal room at one end of the basement. As she got up from finishing her lunch alone, Alice carried two loads of laundry to hang out in the pretty sunshine, on the lines up the hill from the lower part of the yard. As she picked them up to match them with clothespins, Alex's little shirts and shorts tugged at her heart in two ways—for their tiny innocence and for the little message of cold, wet estrangement they seemed to carry.

Below her, down the short steep hill, Daniel's roses still bloomed along one side of the yard, and on the other, his tomatoes were just reaching their crescendo. The grass between those two beds was worn with a grandson's summer of using it every day. She'd complained once to Daniel and he'd asked her, softly, if that was too big a price to pay for all this time with him and Grace. Alice felt herself blush as perhaps she never had before. How could she not have known that? What was it about Grace and her son that shifted her so, that confused her love with worry and fear?

Then she saw him—little Alex—out at the far corner of the yard near where the alley met the road. He was behind the big pine, peeking from behind it as if playing a game, though there was no one else around. Alice caught herself before she called to him, stopped herself from telling him to be careful out there by the street. She hung her next piece of clothing, watching him furtively and wondering if he was doing the same. He looked out from behind the tree again and then walked up the alley to where the walkway through the middle of the back yard met the alley. He stood still there for a moment, looking toward the rose bushes and then at the house. He either did not think to look up the hill or was pretending not to see his grandmother.

He turned and walked back behind the pine then, disappearing for a moment and then emerged again, carrying what Alice thought at first to be some kind of cage he and Daniel had built. It was white and delicately arched. And then, at the moment she knew what it was, she jumped with fright as someone touched her from behind, a pair of arms encircling her just beneath her breast.

"You don't see that boy down there and he doesn't see you," Daniel said. He turned her to face him, smiled at her and then turned her back toward the house. She extended one arm back toward her laundry to protest, and then went easily with him. Daniel steered them not down the hill to the back door, but on into the Sheltons' yard next door and toward the front, so Alex wouldn't see them.

From the kitchen, they watched Alex struggle with the trellis. He seemed to know where he wanted it, but had difficulty setting it exactly as he pushed back the climbing roses on one side and then the other to clear a space. He positioned it several times before he brought the roses back to it, reaching up to place them on the new structure.

"Little man, big plan," Daniel said.

"How can a six-year-old be that careful with flowers?" Alice said.

"Excellent training," Daniel said.

Once satisfied with the trellis, Alex went back to the alley and back behind the tree. Grace came into the kitchen and to the window, standing silently behind her parents. This time Alex continued past the tree and along the side of the road, taking a furtive route to the front just as his grandparents had, but along the other side of the yard.

"What's he doing?" Alice said a few moments after he had disappeared, and as she spoke they could hear him come in the basement door. Soon there was a bump of something against a basement wall, and they stood in silence, waiting to see. Soon he appeared along the street side of the yard again, struggling with dragging two wooden structures that were far too big for him to handle.

When both benches were in place beneath the arc of the trellis, Alex came running straight down the middle of the yard toward the back door. The three adults pulled back quickly from the window, turning to counters and tables as he came in. There was a blindfold first. "It's only for a minute, Grandmother," he told her as he aimed her toward the back door. He began talking about his work even before the little procession had made its way halfway to the end of the yard, long before he asked her to lean down so he could take off the blindfold, before he began explaining about the difference between climbing roses and regular roses.

Sometimes Alice knew she was confused, and took solace in the old wisdom that just knowing the problem was a big step toward conquering it. Every day she thought that, the same way an alcoholic can think every day that this is his last day of drink. And every day she heard people talk about her as if she weren't there, or she saw things she knew but could not remember a use for, or she heard words that jumbled themselves away from real meaning before she could catch hold of them.

In the car, she looked all around her, wanting to see a store she knew. Barnes & Gilley, it was called. Or did it have a new name? She watched and watched, not knowing where she was.

She was on a trip. With Alex. She did not know if he had decided they'd take the trip or she had, but she was glad to be on the trip. She had known about it for a long time, she thought, or had maybe forgotten it and then it had come back, and now they were on their way. It was summertime. They drove toward the sunset as the afternoon faded away, and they rode quietly for a long time while she thought again and again about where they were going and why. She might have asked Alex already or she might not have. Or she might have asked him ten times. What she knew was that the trip was good and that it was for her. She kept thinking she'd see a big bridge, crossing high over something far below and delivering the two of them to something beautiful and quiet and remembered on the other side. And sometimes she thought of ice, and the car skidding and something terrible happening.

Alex spoke to her in the midst of these thoughts. She'd not been able to begin listening quickly enough, and heard only the word "Kentucky."

"What did you say?"

"When was the last time you were back in Kentucky?" he said.

"Oh," she said. She thought of Daniel and of her daughters, and if any one of them might have taken her there. Daniel was dead, she knew, because that was why she had moved to the home. One daughter was dead too—Grace, it was, from an accident. Another daughter had lived so far away for so many years that Alice could not picture her face. The other daughter—Louise was her name—came to the home once a week. In Alice's mind this one daughter had in some way become all three of her daughters. Sweet girls they were, coming every week to see her. Or maybe it was every month. Louise.

A green car came into her view and Alice stopped thinking a moment. She was in a car with someone. With Alex. A man almost as old as the way she remembered Daniel best. "Oh," she said. "Did you say something to me?"

"About Kentucky, you mean?" Alex said. His hands were on top of the steering wheel. Little hands with slender fingers. Little hands she recognized from somewhere. From where they were going, perhaps? The hands were too white to be her daddy's hands.

"Oh yes," she said, hearing about Kentucky. "I remember Kentucky better most days than anything else. I don't know what I did tomorr . . . what I did yesterday, but I remember the little cabin with Daddy and Momma. In the hollow. Dark at three in the afternoon."

"Do you remember that it's all gone now?"

"Kentucky?" Alice said.

"We'll be in Kentucky in a mile or two," Alex said. "The cabin, I mean."

"I remember the cabin," Alice told him. "It was cold. Momma got angry."

"Do you know what we'll see?" Alex said.

She did not, and had no answer for him. She looked out ahead of them and thought hard about Kentucky. Something about Kentucky and a car made her hands feel cold and wet. She looked down at her hands. There were little pieces of paper under them, on her lap. Some of the pieces of paper had pictures on them. She looked up quickly again and then at the man driving the car, not wanting to look at the pictures just then. Then she looked down again, frowning. She picked up one of them to look at it harder.

She heard the driver's voice and knew it was Alex. He said something about a handsome man. Alice asked him what he'd just said.

"Your daddy was a handsome man."

She looked at the photograph. It was small and dirty and dark looking and it was hard for her eyes to make it into a picture. "Daddy," she said, and handed the picture to Alex.

"You have more there," Alex said. "Our pictures for the trip."

Alice handed him another one. He put it out in front of him above the steering wheel. "Your daughters were beautiful on this day too," he said. She looked at him and reached for the picture. Three women were standing by a tree, with shorts on, in the summer time. She looked hard at it and handed it back to Alex. Then she reached down and picked up the rest of the pictures in her lap and handed them all to him.

"You don't want to look at them?" he said.

"It's going to be dark," she said.

"You left one more there in your lap," he said.

She looked down at her hands. The oldest hands she'd ever seen. There was no picture on the little piece of paper near her hands. She picked it up, and Alex told her to turn it over.

"You know who took that?" he said.

She looked at the paper again. "Nobody took it," she said. "I have it right here."

"Turn it over," he said again, and reached for her hand. He took the piece of paper for just a second and then gave it back to her. There was a picture there. "That one's not so long ago for you, but a long long time ago for me," he said. "That's the first picture I ever took, with the first camera I ever had. You know who that is, sitting there under the roses?"

Alice looked. "It's Louise," she said. She didn't know for sure, but she was glad to have an answer for him.

Alex laughed. "It looks like Louise," he said. "It's you, Grandma. It's you in the backyard at the old house, the day Dandad and I built the trellis out there and took you out to show it to you."

Alice looked down at the picture. She remembered something. "Alex was six then," she said. She looked outside at the trees going by as they went up a hill. She felt a chill of something terrible again. "Grace was six," she said, "in the car that day." She looked down at the picture again. "I was six," she thought next, wondering if she had said it. "I was six and sitting on the step when Daddy came home. Momma was angry but I didn't care. In Kentucky. I was six. It got dark early and you could see the moon. We'll see the big full Kentucky moon as soon as it gets dark up ahead, Alex. Soon as it gets dark."

Motherless Children

It was this way: She died in October, somewhere so deep into the night that she was not fully awake when she got up to use the bathroom and then fell. Fell to her death. Her husband, who lived only a year and nine days after that night, was awakened by the horrible noise of her crash into the plumbing. She was seventy years old, healthy, a daily gardener and walker, a wife, a mother and a grandmother. Grace, her name was, as if her mother had known who she'd grow into being. She would have lived another twenty-five years, based on her mother's and one of her grandmothers' lives, but during her last eight or ten she would have drifted; would have become confused and unmoored from the specifics of her life and would have had moments of speaking pleasantly with people who weren't there just then. Instead there was a gruesome crushed-in wound to her head, a coma, three weeks of hopes built on tiny twitches of the eye, and then merciful death. She must have stumbled on the flimsy bathmat, was her husband's theory. Or perhaps there was an aneurysm or heart attack or other internal tragedy before she fell. The death was a shock to the people she knew. Among the group she hiked with, the reaction was this: She was so young, so active, so involved—the leader among her age peers and people twenty years younger. She left two sons—middle-aged men who'd stayed by her side in the hospital till her end, and an ex-husband who regretted the loss of her now for a second time.

Or this way: After she lost a daughter to mental illness and a son to a river when he was sixteen and she was fifty-two, Grace never fully recovered. She'd already divorced Edwin—for repeated infidelities, over a period of perhaps ten years, with the same woman—and had remarried, to an abrasive, loud man who was nevertheless gracious, and likely faithful, to her. She took up with him initially because of no more than his blustery demand that she do so, and she had no intention of staying with a man who spoke too loudly, who was talked about behind his back, who was estranged not only from his first wife but also two of his three daughters. But then little Cannon drowned, tumbling from a canoe on a river where he shouldn't have been in the first place. Sixteen, he was, out with a friend who knew the river; the next day they were to go to West Virginia, where Cannon was to teach the other boy to climb rocks. The river boy survived the water and Cannon did not. The man Grace married, within three months of the drowning, was a rum drinker, and he began to work at soothing Grace's pain each day just after noon. Within a few years after they married, they were both slurred and stumbling by six P.M.—he full of foolish, noisy, overblown convictions and certainties and she equally oversupplied with joyous proclamations built on slight misconnections, as if determined to counter her partner's admonitions to all to *just understand just one thing.* Her death was a long slow process which only coincidentally culminated in her own bathroom.

Or it was this way, deep into that night in the house out

in the country where they lived alone: Drunk, as they were each evening, they fought on this particular night. Kelvey, fully impotent for more than ten years, nonetheless on occasion demanded Grace's efforts with him. For several years before he'd fully traded alcohol for the functioning of his body, she had indulged him for long, nearly always fruitless sessions on their sheets; and for the beginning of those years he'd been thankful and gracious to her. But there was an increasing meanness borne of his own certainty about what had happened to him and his need to deny the cause, and so at times he took it out on her. Four times after he had passed the age of sixty-five, he told her there was nothing she could do to stop him if he took all the money they had, left her and found a younger woman, with younger parts. She comforted herself that he never said such things when he was sober. And on their best days—on a hiking trail at nine in the morning and with three or four hours ahead of them before they began their daily descent—she could look at him and like him, could remember when they met, when she was forty-nine and he was fifty-two. There had been a time when she might have fallen in love with him. There had been a time when he looked after her backpack, made sure he rode with her in the carpools to hikes, bought her dinner that evening. He'd been nearly a boy with her. There had been the deep illness of her daughter and now the loss of her son, and things became rushed and jumbled and clouded, and the next thing she knew, she had been married to him for fifteen years, and worked each morning to make things good and shiny, and failed each afternoon as the first pieces of shadow began to come into the house across her throw rugs.

The boy in the river. He moved his life too fast, wanting to try everything that was outdoors. After his sophomore year in high school, he and the brother of the friend he would go into the river with started west on bicycles—heading out the national road through Western Maryland. On a sharp turn two days into the trip, an Atlas Moving Van came across the road and hit them both. The bicycles—new, carefully researched before purchase, and offering the best technology available in the 1970s—were smashed beyond repair. The friend was left with both legs broken and a gash that would leave a scar on his face the rest of his life. Cannon, who had planned the trip, ordered all the maps, learned about bicycles, who had ridden a hundred miles each weekend for the previous three months—that boy came away with nothing but abrasions. But they were deep and pervasive, completely stripping skin from one side of one leg, the back of one arm and the trunk flesh from his armpit to a strange, two-inch gap before the leg wound began its way down to the side of his foot. He spent one day under his mother's care—or at least until her new, there-all-evening-every-day boyfriend arrived after work when he retreated to his room—and then began to force himself to move around, to get ready to go back outside as soon as he could. He began to plan more local things for his summer. Canoeing a fast river, for one.

Or this: There were deep wounds from his parents' divorce, which took place when he was eight—maybe the perfect age to know that it is your own fault that the most important thing you knew shatters in front of you. And so he grew up reckless, growing his own marijuana plants beginning when he was thirteen. Cutting school when there was something better to do. He kept his grades, for both his parents' sake and for his own, but somewhere farther in him than school performance was an anger that came out in big physical movement. He became a rock climber and a skier, a cross country cyclist and lone hiker. On excursions with his age peers, he was the one to lead, the one to take the risk. And once Kelvey came along, another strand of attachment broke loose within him. He had never told himself his mother and father would get back together; after all, his father lived with the woman who'd caused the problems. Cannon didn't hate her, exactly—she was smart and kind and occasionally almost apologetic—but she sometimes touched a small wound in him. It was a wound that no more than the simple sight of Kelvey tore open again and again. Cannon looked for more reasons to leave, more trips to take, a place deep in the woods to grow his plants. He never raised his voice to his mother until Kelvey came, and then it happened once a week. He was angry. Looking for risk and danger.

Or it was an accident, pure and simple. Even with the portend—the truck, driven by a man used to interstates and sent instead into the mountains of Western Maryland—it was simply a set of circumstances that met at one time and one place, as happens with every accident. The trucker lost control, felt a second of relief that there were no cars in the oncoming lane, and then watched as the bicycles and the boys bounced off his big rig into the air and then back to the road surface. The river was more preventable, but still an accident. Cannon had made his own decisions about where he went in the great outdoors since he was twelve. He hiked with one parent or the other from time to time—in hiking groups full of older people—or he went with friends or he went alone. The brother of the broken cyclist was a one-time river guide in West Virginia, at nineteen years old. Cannon was ready to learn the Potomac, swollen though it was from rains. They went on a gray, swirl-clouded Saturday morning, driving through rain and wind in April to the river. The nineteen-year-old had the canoes, the knowledge, the strength. The sixteen year-old hit a pocket just over a rock; he came out of the boat, went under, hit a rock, and he was gone. He might have ridden the same stretch a thousand times and never hit that same little set of circumstances again.

And too there was a sister. Out of high school, she went away to New York City, carrying her perfect grades, her keen sense of literature and art with her to college in 1969. Her family did not see her for four months, from September to Christmas, and then she came home someone else. She came home haunted by someone she called Francoise. A fellow student? her family asked. No, she said. A teacher? A townie? A staff person? Irritated, she at last said Francoise was all of those things and so much more that she could not even describe. Francoise was God, Lisa said another day, and who was anyone in her family to even ask? She went back to school the day after Christmas, in a manner that seemed designed to spite those she'd visited, those she'd lived with all her life. She refused a car drive, a ride to the airport or the train station. Dressed in a frilled, suede, men's leather smoking jacket far too large for her, she went out in front of the house—a small residential street in a neighborhood of small, identical houses built for war workers in the '40s—and put her thumb too high into the air, on a street where no one but her parents' neighbors drove.

In the largest sense, she never came home again. Within a month after that, her family learned later, she was no longer enrolled. She moved to a commune just away from the campus. Her mother and older brother went to visit her that spring, and on her own new turf, Lisa was softer, less determined to hate them. There's a place for you here too, she said. At least the two of you if not everyone else back there, she said, though Francoise and Dia Babba both say that all are welcomed. She spoke quickly, as if there were something else she needed to get to right then. She sat on the floor as she spoke, her legs crossed in front of her and her body rocking, just slightly, forward and back from the waist. She was thin, with strong acne and long, unwashed hair. Francoise and Dia Babba cared for all, she said. Francoise didn't live there, Lisa told her mother with an impatience that indicated she should already have known this, but her spirit was always there. Always. Grace and Alex went back home with the clothing and food and belongings they had taken to her.

There were twenty more years for Lisa. Years that were both as fast as the years of a child who's yours and as elongated as those for someone you watch each day with knowledge of a terminal illness. She lived in New York State, briefly in California and Colorado over those years, moving at first from commune to commune and then from marginal downtown neighborhood to broken downtown neighborhood to dark and dangerous downtown neighborhood. In her California years—in Berkeley and then Oakland—she was first diagnosed with schizophrenia and later with AIDS. For the last years she lived alone or with string-haired men who beat her or helped her drug herself or sold her. One year, from what seemed out of nowhere, she contacted her younger brother Brian, telling him she wanted to come East again, to try living with him since he had remained single all his life. Brian was startled, slightly unmoored, but he told her yes. You can look back on so much and see it for what it was, or for what people take it for once it's occurred: She came home to die, to do the best she could to readmit herself to the people who'd raised her and the brothers who'd teased her. The roommates idea failed, and within two months after moving to a downtown Baltimore neighborhood indistinguishable from the last ten places she had lived, she was dead.

How could they have known, Grace and Edwin, when they set out under those crystalline blue skies that shone so brightly just after the war that the color would blind them if they saw it now? Edwin was twenty-eight, and so shimmering with love for his new wife that he sometimes could scarcely breathe. Grace stood him up once, as he waited forlorn and alone—had his own mother known something when she decided not to come to the wedding?—at the altar, six months before they finally did marry. She'd known his vulnerability and perhaps seen it as a weakness. Why marry a man who wanted her so desperately? But finally, perhaps weighing her mother's adamant wishes that she not, she wed Edwin Hardin and started her new life near Baltimore, just down the road from the aircraft plant where they had worked during the war, an event that had lifted up and away from the world with such huge suddenness and emotion as to create a sort of vacuum, into which the dreams and love and joy of people like Edwin and Grace were sucked so fast and ferociously that many never saw it happen, didn't know the forces that moved them onward.

So it was that children came in the wave that still cascades through the demographics. Three of them born between '46 and '51. Alex. Lisa. Brian. And then the surprise Edwin, Jr. just before the sixties, when clouds had already begun to change the quality of the blue above them all. Cannon, his mother called him immediately and forever. And what would they have done, Grace and Edwin, if somehow they *could* have known then what the three Hardins still left now know? With Brian living alone with a dog and an endless string of small green Rolling Rock bottles, as if their tiny size somehow makes them less a threat to his health. Sometimes he'll tell you he's killing himself seven ounces at a time. But then who's to say some of us aren't going faster than that? he'll say next, and laugh.

Motherless children they all three are: A man moving past ninety and approaching at last the wisdom to visit the injustices he did his wife, to taste remorse over his own mother, who died two thousand miles away from him while living with a brother he seldom speaks to; his only brother, also past eighty, living near the Rockies. Edwin lives alternately with a large woman and alone amid the clutter of his life, telling others and himself what he's said all his life: He's about to clean it all up.

The two remaining sons are becoming old men, and spend only hours together each year. They stood together for several weeks to watch their mother while the last gallons of her reservoir of strength kept her alive as one chemical addiction was replaced with even stronger pain killers. They cried for her, for themselves. They stood next to her, read to her and told her things from her life.

How long does it take to be able to wonder, to try to understand the death of your own mother, your sister, your brother? How long does it take before you can go to that place in your mind and heart where they once lived and have not now for so long, and bear to stay there for more than the three seconds it takes to remember the little symbol of them that your mind has adopted, its shorthand a sort of antiseptic for a wound that never heals? They all three knock softly on the doors of the three who remain; and then stand behind it, speaking with an aching muteness, in tones meant not for understanding but to convey some blend of question and accusation, of anger and anguish, spoken from a place you cannot see, through a door that won't open.

I. Saw My Mother Today

She drove into the parking lot next door at work, in an old tan Plymouth as big as an airplane—right up next to the building where people get out and take their dogs inside to be clipped and dipped. It was not the kind of car my mother ever drove, and she never owned a dog, but there she was in the car—small, tidy, short-haired, efficient-looking. She was no older, and perhaps even slightly younger, than I remember her, from the years when she was healthy and strong.

I watched for the Plymouth to stop, but it drove on through the lot and toward the back lot of the dog place. I went outside into the winter weather my mother always loved, to look for the tan Plymouth. I walked all the way around the pet service shop, and then I went inside to ask about the Plymouth. I had looked from my window over into their lobby many times over the years, but had never been in. It smelled faintly of animals yet to be cleaned and preened. The pet people checked with each other and said they hadn't noticed the big tan Plymouth.

At home, I told my wife I'd seen my mother drive by

my window at work, in a big tan Plymouth. Janet smiled and absently patted at my arm, much as my mother might have done decades ago, when I was a boy telling her a wild story and she was a pretty young woman busy folding laundry.

One of my mother's grandsons, so young as to remember her only vaguely, came into the house then and asked me if we still had a Scrabble game.

"I remember," he said absently as we went to the shelf full of boxed games, "playing once with, um, with your mother—back when I must have hardly known any words." When I asked him what had made him think of the game today, he said he wasn't really sure, but it might have been something in English class. We put the old purple box onto the dining room table. Seventeen and usually hurried, he paused as he held the top of the box, wherein personal high scores had been recorded for decades. Then he looked up. "Clouding up majorly," he said, looking toward the window that revealed a deepening winter gray. He turned back to the blonde-wood tiles, all face down and all in little rows. A tiny army of unseen letters at the ready.

Another grandson, in through the back door, walked toward the table and then looked back toward the door, as if he'd forgotten something.

"Welsh rarebit!" he called out, "Tomato soup and cheese over cracks." Twenty and given to fancy cooking or nothing else in the kitchen, he opened two cans of tomato soup and scouted for saltines. He undrawered a bone-handled knife my grandmother had once given to my mother, and sliced even, thin pieces of cheese. He monitored the flame under the soup as he dropped in pieces of cheese and then spread crackers on plates. "Serious youth deja vu," he said.

The third of the brothers—fifteen—walked slowly

across the back yard. At the table, we paused as our lunch was readied and looked up. He stopped, still far out into the yard, and pointed in toward us.

"He's trying to tell us something," Janet said.

"Gee," said the rarebit boy, "she figured that out in a hurry." Between the boy in the yard and the window was the bird feeder, a long-ago Christmas gift from their grandmother, neglected for perhaps a decade after a squirrel takeover in its first winter of use. Finches and wrens and sparrows flitted there now, working hard at seeds.

The boy of fifteen came in, a scent of cold about him. "It's going to snow," he said.

"It's a big front, moving fast," said my mother's oldest grandson, much taller now than she ever was.

"Up from Texas," said the middle boy. "Where all the big snows come from. It's supposed to get here within an hour."

"Who filled the bird feeder?" said Janet.

Boys looked at each other with opened eyes and flattened palms as people watched birds and the cook ladled cheesy red sauce for the late arrival.

"Who's playing Scrabble?" said the fifteen-year-old.

"You know who loved that game?" said the second-eldest.

"Grandma Grace," two people said at the same time.

"Remember the time she had us all at her place for like a week, when we were all like four or five or something?" said the cook. "And hotshot over there was in diapers? She had all these weather books and insect books and stuff."

"We had that long bird list and we planted trees," said the middle boy, blond and thin.

"White pines," said the eldest.

Janet was at the freezer just then, seeking coffee beans. She pulled out an old metal ice tray. The sectioning was not in it, and so what was inside the tray was one long frozen block, a yellow-orange color. She asked what it was.

"It's Three Fives," said the middle grandson. "Or Five Threes. I can't remember which."

"You made it?" Janet said.

"No, the Good Humor man delivered it earlier, despite it being seriously out of season for him and his bell froze up."

"But how did you know," Janet paused, looking around, "what's in it?"

"Three cups each of like orange juice, water, banana, sugar and lemon juice," he said. "Or pretty close anyway."

"Where'd you get the recipe?" said the eldest.

"Just sort of came to me," was the reply, as Janet reached for bowls and scooped big portions into them. As she slid them across the same paths the Welsh rarebit plates had traveled, the first flakes of snow fell out by the bird feeder. Big flakes. Boys sat quietly with bowls and spoons, looking at tiles or out the window at the gathering snow and evening. No one said he had a friend to meet. No one needed to go to a ball game. Or had a girl to call or go see. The house felt closed down, isolated, protected as night came. People helped each other find words in the Scrabble game. Snow fell fatter and harder. Birds flitted at the feeder as if working to keep the seed free of snow. The Five Threes was as smooth and sweet as when I'd eaten it as a boy.

I saw my mother today.

KURT RHEINHEIMER's short stories have appeared in more than 60 periodicals, ranging from *Redbook* and *Playgirl* to *Michigan Quarterly Review* and *Glimmer Train*. His stories have been anthologized in four volumes of *New Stories from the South: The Year's Best*, from Algonquin Books. His first short story collection, *Little Criminals* (Eastern Washington University Press, 2005), won the Spokane Prize for Fiction, was reviewed favorably in *The New York Times Review of Books* and was a finalist for Virginia Fiction Book of the Year in 2006. Kurt lives with his wife Gail in Roanoke, Virginia, where he has been editor in chief at Leisure Publishing (*The Roanoker, Blue Ridge Country, Virginia Travel Guide* and many other publications) since 1984.

Cover artist MATT HUNTER is a Senior Game Software Developer, ultramarathoner, and amateur photographer living in Nova Scotia, Canada.

Find more of his photography at www.flickr.com/photos/technologyrocks/.

APR -- 2014

CPSIA information can be obtained at www.ICGtesting.com
Printed in the USA
BVOW020302240412
288428BV00001B/2/P

9 781935 708582